AIA
THE
BARBARIAN

Mark O'Bannon

Published by MEOw Publishing.

Visit our website at: www.MEOwPublishing.com

First published in 2024

ISBN 978-1-933888-20-0

Printed in the United States of America

This book is dedicated to the cover artist,
whose painting inspired me to write this story:

Lorenzo Sperlonga

Books by Mark O'Bannon

IMPERIUM PREQUEL SERIES
(May be read in any order)
Pirates of the Imperium
High Salvage
Touching Infinity

IMPERIUM SERIES
Imperium – Return of the Archons (Coming in 2026)

SHADOWS & DREAMS SERIES
The Dream Crystal
The Dark Mirrors of Heaven (Coming in 2026)

AIA THE BARBARIAN SERIES
Aia the Barbarian – The Fallen God

WHISKERS
Whiskers (Coming in 2025)

CONTENTS

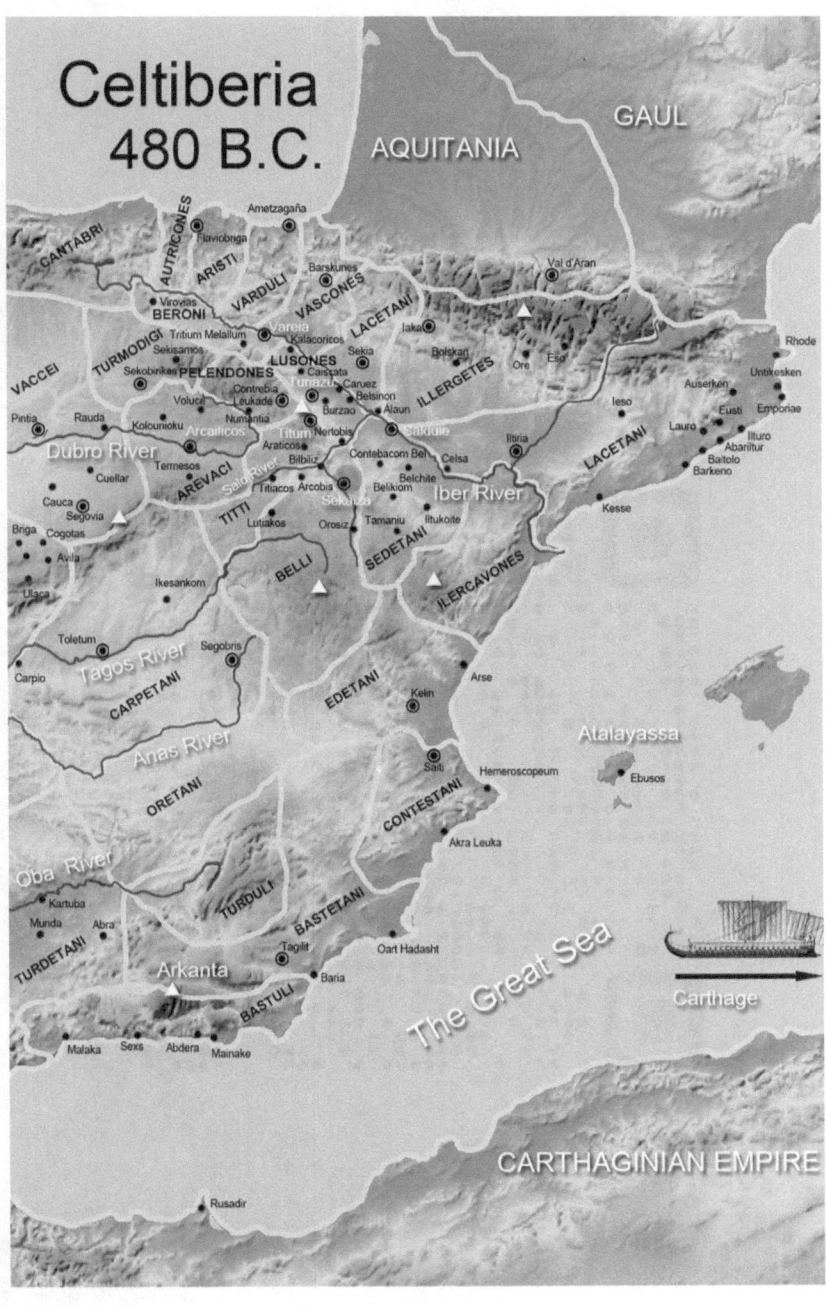

Celtiberia
480 B.C.

GAUL

AQUITANIA

CANTABRI

AUTRIGONES

Ametzagaña

Flaviobriga

ARISTI

VARDULI

Barskunes

Val d'Aran

Viroviās

BERONI

VASCONES

LACETANI

Iaka

Rhode

TURMODIGI

Tritium Melallum

Vareia

Kalacoricos

Sekia

Bolskan

Elso

Ore

Auserken

Untixesken

Sekisamos

LUSONES

Caraspata

Emporiae

VACCEI

Sekobirikes

PELENDONES

Contrebia

Caruez

Belsinon

ILLERGETES

Ieso

Eusti

Voluce

Leukade

Tumazita

Burzao

Alaun

Lauro

Pintia

Rauda

Koloumoku

Numantia

Titum

Nertobis

Salduie

Ituro

Abaniltur

Arcailicos

Araticos

Contebacom Bel

Celsa

Iltiria

Baitolo

Dubro River

Bilbiliz

LACETANI

Barkeno

Termesos

Belchite

Kesse

Cuellar

AREVACI

Salo River

Titiacos

Arcobia

Belkiom

Iber River

Cauca

Sekaiza

Segovia

TITTI

Lutiakos

Orosiz

Tamaniu

Iltukoite

Briga

Cogotas

BELLI

SEDETANI

Avila

Ikesankom

ILERCAVONES

Ulaca

Toletum

Tagos River

Segobris

Carpio

CARPETANI

EDETANI

Arse

Kelin

Anas River

ORETANI

Saiti

Hemeroscopeum

Atalayassa

Ebusos

CONTESTANI

Akra Leuka

Oba River

Kartuba

TURDULI

Munda

Abra

BASTETANI

Tegilt

Oart Hadasht

TURDETANI

Arkanta

Baria

BASTULI

The Great Sea

Malaka

Sexs

Abdera

Mainake

CARTHAGINIAN EMPIRE

Carthage

Rusadir

Go To:
www.MEOwPublishing.com
to see a high quality map of Celtiberia

"If the radiance of a thousand suns were to burst at once in the sky, that would be like the splendor of the Mighty One."

— *Bhagavad Gita, Chapter 11, Verse 12"*

CHAPTER ONE
The Vanquished

To the north, far beyond the walls of the shining city of Carthage are the lands of heroes long-forgotten. Keltoi kingdoms lay across Iberia like stars burning in the darkness—Ilercavones, Edetani, Bastetani, Turdetani, the Tartessians who came from Atlantis after their realm sank beneath the waves, Lusitania the land of priests and sorcerers, the Celtici with their fair-haired women, the Carpetani who guard the secret of steel, the Aquitanians who dwell in the mountains and by the sea, the cruel Sedetani who love warfare as much as wine, and the Callæci whose great tower guards against giants from beyond the edge of the world. The greatest among these peoples are the Celtiberians who surround their lands with a ring of fortresses. A girl named Aia, sharp, quick-witted and graceful, had a destiny to fulfill. Here is a tale of a barbarian. . . .

— The Chronicles of Aristæus

Sacred birds whirled and swirled and twirled about the blue sky, circling in silence. One by one, they came down to snatch a soul belonging to a man of valor. With a flap of air the birds would take off again, scintillating in the golden sunlight, engulfed in the flame of the soul they carried up to heaven.

A vulture landed close by, whipping up the smell of rotting flesh. Aia lay on the battlefield among the glorious dead, benumbed and staring into the blue sky. A trickle of blood dripped into her eyes. Blinking, she remained still, inhaling defeat. A broken army lay about her, slaughtered.

Aia whispered, "Oh, Karbelos my love, where are you now?"

Lazy hoof beats approached. Numbness was a blanket that quenched the flames of fury. Aia let the fire in her heart die down to a glowing ember and lay still. At the head of a hundred Iberian cavalrymen, two of the conquerors rode into view. One wore a gold Celtic helmet with intricate engravings on the crown and cheek guards. The other man was bare-chested and well muscled. Covered with sweat and blood, he had the look of an animal. Wearing no helmet, his long dark hair fell about his shoulders in a wild entanglement. Fire burned in his eyes, incinerating the world around him.

Aia stopped blinking.

The bare-chested man spoke first, "We have crushed our enemies."

The man with the gold helmet nodded. "Yes, lord Culchas. Twenty thousand of the Lusones lay here, dead. It is a great victory, though their king has escaped."

Chuckling, Culchas matched his companion's smile. "Olónico is powerless. Now, Turiazu has no army to protect its walls." His gaze swept over the corpses surrounding Aia and his eyes halted when they came to her.

Aia held her breath.

Culchas admired Aia for a moment. Long blonde hair fell in curls halfway down her back. She wore animal skins and little else, except for a pair of Celtic swords, one long and the other short. "Their women are as beautiful as they are brave. We should have captured more of them, Orisos. The Carthaginians pay well for slaves."

"The gateway to paradise is under the shade of swords," chanted Orisos, "Neito has been good to us today." He smiled after invoking the name of the Iberian war god. "We have enough of them already."

Culchas laughed. "You're right, Orisos. Tonight, after we sacrifice their leaders, we shall drink their wine and bed their women!"

Numbness became a smoldering fire once again. Aia let the air slip out of her lungs.

With a gesture, Culchas summoned a man from his escort—a rider with a bow. He pointed in Aia's direction. "Kill that one."

The rider raised his bow and pointed it at Aia. Before she could react, the arrow flew through the air. Aia braced herself.

The vulture beside her screeched and collapsed across her chest, dead. Aia exhaled in relief and watched the column of men ride past. They had descended from the fallen citadel perched atop a high bluff above the town. Burzao had fallen to the invaders. The soldiers rode on, raising a cloud of dust into the air as they passed down into the valley below the hill of bodies.

Moving like a cat, Aia used the natural smoke screen to cover her progress while she searched the dead. After a time, she found what she was looking for. The man lay on his back with a spear in his chest. Aia ran a gentle finger down his cheek, whispering to her friend, "Goodbye Tarbantu." Reaching behind him, Aia unfastened a pendant holding a piece of steel from around his neck and she put

3

it around hers. Closing her eyes, Aia invoked a silent prayer to Epona so that the goddess would escort her friend to the underworld.

A rough hand grabbed her shoulder.

"It is dishonorable to steal from the dead." Although the words were in the Celtiberian tongue, there was a heavy Iberian accent. Aia felt herself being spun around. She looked into a pair of grinning eyes.

The Sedetani soldier punched her in the face. A flash of pain exploded in her cheek.

Aia fell to the ground.

Laughter.

Another man spoke in the Iberian language. "Don't leave any marks on her Turibas. I want to play with her before we throw her in the cage."

Half a dozen men were standing behind Turibas, surrounded by the dead army. One of the soldiers slit the throat of a wounded man. Aia narrowed her eyes, simmering in defiance. She began to rise.

Turibas placed the sharp point of a spear against her chest. "I found her," he grinned, "so I'll take her." He called out to his companions, "A slave needs to be broken in first."

His companions chuckled.

Distracted by their laughter, he looked away for a moment.

With one smooth motion, Aia knocked his spear out of the way and while drawing her short Celtic sword, she slashed out, rolling to the side. By the time she leapt to her feet, Turibas lay on the ground, bleeding.

The nearest man cursed and came at her.

Aia sidestepped his spear thrust and moved forward, slashing. Her short sword struck him in the side and he fell to the ground. She caught another man off guard and he went down with a quick slash.

The four remaining soldiers stood nearby, hesitating.

Moving the short sword into her left hand, Aia drew a long Celtic sword from the sheath over her back. Now she held a sword in each hand. Her words were in Celtiberian. "Come on," she smiled, "play with me."

With a shout one soldier ran forward, thrusting his spear.

Aia parried the spear with her short sword, stepped inside his guard and slashed him in the chest. As he went down, screaming, another man leapt forward, sword in hand.

Aia twirled around, dodging his blow and struck him in the back of the head with the pommel of her short sword. Though it hit his iron helmet, he went down anyway. Blood flowed from underneath the dent in the helm.

The last two men were more cautious. They looked at each other, waiting for the other man to move first.

Aia attacked. Sprinting forward, she struck one adversary in the chest with her sword before he could block it. Out of the corner of her eye she saw the last man throw his spear. She ducked the long shaft and faced him down. The man drew a mace and advanced with caution.

With a shout, Aia rushed him, striking at once with both swords. He managed to block one of them but the second blow hit him in the face. He went down.

Aia shook her head, muttering aloud, "So much for sneaking around."

The numbness had given way to a headache, no doubt from the scratch on her head. Pausing long enough to clean her two swords, she looked out away from the battlefield, towards freedom, but a nagging curiosity pulled her eyes back. Her gaze swept back through the enemy encampment while a mischievous thought came to mind.

A smile touched her lips: She was a girl plotting mischief.

* * *

Holding a bloody cloth to her forehead, Aia strode into the chamber where a dozen girls sat on imported Persian carpets laid between the columns that supported the archways of the building. A few girls were still trying to remove their chains, to no avail. The clinking of metal stopped when Aia came in. Silent now, the prisoners looked into her eyes, defiant.

Aia couldn't help but admire them. She smiled.

A Sedetani soldier stepped inside, halting at the sight of Aia.

Before he could say anything, Aia called out to him in perfect Iberian, "You there! I'd like a word with you."

The guard glanced over his shoulder and moved closer, raising his eyebrows.

Aia motioned towards a nearby table which held a pitcher and several earthenware cups for visitors. "Bring me a cup of wine."

He looked at the cloth she held to her forehead. "Are you alright?"

"How very good of you to ask." She removed the cloth and tossed it onto a table made of carved oak. "The swordsman who gave me this scratch is lying next to his friends up on the hill." She nodded towards the dead army of the Lusones.

The man went over to retrieve a cup and pouring wine into it, came back.

Aia thanked him with her eyes and drank down the wine. The cool draught sent a chill through her body, invigorating her. Aia let a coy smile play on her lips.

The man returned the smile.

Aia handed him back the cup. "Is the sergeant of the guard here?"

"Yes, he's just outside," said the soldier. "Is there a problem?"

"Are you stationed here to guard these slaves?"

"Yes."

Gathering storm clouds slipped into her voice, "You're the problem! Go get the sergeant of the guard now."

The man nearly dropped the cup, hesitating.

A thunderbolt: "Now!"

A grin spread across her face as the guard went out.

A moment later, the sergeant of the guard stood in front of Aia while the newly captured slave girls looked on. "What is it, woman?"

Disdainful, Aia looked down her nose. "Are you in charge here?"

"Yes. Who are you?"

"My name is Aia. I'm a member of the royal guard." She motioned towards the captives. "These are the most beautiful girls among all of the slaves we've taken, are they not?"

"Yes, they're being held under guard here until the king has finished feasting."

Aia crossed her arms. "Tell me sergeant, how can a girl like me just walk right in here without anyone asking questions?"

The sergeant began to speak, but stopped himself just as quickly.

"This is a high security area, isn't it?"

"Yes, of course it is."

Aia sighed. "I shall have your names. You'll be disciplined for this." She glanced at the first guard, shaking her head. "This man gave me a cup of wine! I can't believe it!"

The sergeant glanced at his companion with ire. "You gave her a cup?"

Aia chose to press her advantage. "This place has the worst security in the army. I suppose you haven't even brought up the wagons yet?"

"Wagons?"

Aia huffed. "How do you think I'm supposed to transport these slaves back to the capital? Salduie is a long way."

"I haven't received any orders."

Aia put her hands on her hips. "General Orisos asked me to take these slaves to the capital tonight. How can I do that without wagons?"

"I'll need a signed order before I can release—"

"All right then, why don't you walk right into the feast and ask the general to write everything down for you. I'm sure he won't mind that you've detained an officer of the king." Aia waved her hand at the sergeant. "Go ahead, I'll wait here."

The sergeant looked askance at the other guard. "Bring up some wagons—with provisions for four days."

* * *

Aia glanced over her shoulder at the high bluff overlooking Burzao and at the mountains beyond. The green hills had given way to brown with the approach of summer. She traveled along the road southeast to Belsinon in the direction of Salduie beyond. A contingent of Sedetani soldiers marched in the opposite direction up the road. More than a few of them whistled at the slave girls inside the cage.

Once the soldiers had passed, a girl in the back of the wagon spoke in broken Iberian. "Who are you?"

Aia glanced over her shoulder inside the cage and replied in Celtiberian. "My name is Aia."

8

The girl had a look of surprise in her face. "You're not Sede-tani?"

Aia shook her head. "I am one of the Arevaci."

The slave girls all began to speak at once.

Aia glanced around, hoping no one would hear their commo-tion. When they'd calmed down, Aia asked, "What's your name?"

"Katulatin," said the girl. "Where are you taking us?"

Not bothering to turn around this time, Aia smiled. "Where would you like to go?"

Katulatin laughed in relief. "Take us west to Turiazu."

Aia shook her head. "We won't reach Turiazu in time—not before the Sedetani army." She turned around to look through the bars. "How about Caiscata?"

Katulatin's smile faded away.

The stillness of the countryside was broken by a distant rumble.

Aia saw more than a hundred children emerging from the crest of the hill on the left side of the road. They were running, terrified. Aia halted the wagon. A rumbling noise came from over the hill, growing louder. Aia stood up, listening and recognized the sound of galloping horses. More than twenty chariots appeared over the crest of the hill. The swift chariots bore down on the children.

As they neared their prey, the charioteers loosed arrows or hurled javelins. One by one, children went down, screaming. The charioteers were treating it like a game, seeing who could catch and kill the most.

Katulatin shouted, "Do something!"

Aia sat down. There was no chance of her defeating so many men.

A boy about the age of eight was just about to cross the road in front of the wagon when a chariot rode up behind him. The laughing charioteer threw a javelin. The boy fell down in the road, impaled in the back. Blood pooled in the road and spilled into the fading sunlight.

Not knowing what to say, Aia muttered, "Who am I to stop them?"

Katulatin rasped, "You are nothing!"

* * *

The white city appeared as the boat came around a bend in the river. A horn sounded a greeting from a tower. Arcailicos was a fortress city by the Dubro River, with a white stone bridge leading to the main gate, overlooking the water a hundred feet below. Arcailicos, full of waterfalls and flowers, was the most beautiful place Aia had ever seen. But Arcailicos had recently undergone some changes: It was being transformed into a foreign city—a "polis." She frowned at the foreign word, wishing that the king would go back to their old ways.

The slaves had all gone, having fled into the countryside on the other side of the mountains. None had chosen to accompany Aia on her journey. Now, the slaves were like wolf cubs lost in the wilderness. For a moment Aia wondered if it was a cruel thing, helping them to escape, but she realized that they had to choose their own paths, even if it led them to darker fates.

Aia disembarked from the boat and went up a stone staircase leading to the bridge. Mists rose into the air, covering the stone with dampness. The sun gave little warmth to Aia as she passed over the river. Moving through the city, Aia noticed stonemasons finishing up the day's work on an amphitheater. The foreigners walked away into the fading light, heading home.

A little girl sat on the steps leading up to the palace, holding a doll. Aia sat down. Taking the necklace from around her neck,

Aia handed it to the girl. "The battle is lost, but your father was an honorable man, Aunia. He helped King Olónico escape."

The little girl took the necklace, gazing into Aia's eyes. Before Aia could say anything more, the girl ran off, unwilling to let the world see her tears. Aia leaned back on the stone steps and allowed a sigh to escape her lips.

Aia's eyes drifted over to the marble courtyard in front of the palace. A dozen heads decorated spears overlooking the public square. Aia was glad to have missed whatever speech preceded their execution. Examining them, she wondered what their offenses were, until her eyes met the face of a friend.

Burning with rage, Aia stormed into the palace. A pair of twelve foot high oak doors stood at the threshold to the king's council chamber. They were each carved with the image of a cherry tree and had knotwork running around the edges. Two guards, holding spears, stood outside.

Ignoring the fire in her heart, Aia slowed down a pace and, smiling at one of the guards, strolled up to the doorway. The man to one side of the door looked into her eyes. Stepping close, Aia ran a finger over his bare arm and up to his chest. "Hello Arbiskar." She threw a glance at the other man and asked in a breathy voice, "Is this one of your friends?"

Arbiskar grinned. "He's not important."

The other man scowled. Aia wrinkled her nose, stepped behind Arbiskar and put her arms around his shoulders. "No?"

"Forget him."

Aia leaned her head against Arbiskar's back. In a distracted tone she asked, "What's going on inside?"

"The king is holding a council meeting."

"Mind if I take a peek?"

Arbiskar frowned. "What would you want to look in there for?"

She whispered in his ear, "Please?"

With an audible sigh, Arbiskar cracked open the door. "Be quick about it."

The second guard shook his head, grinning at Arbiskar.

Before they could stop her, Aia slipped through the doorway.

King Caros stood overlooking a table where a roll of papyrus had been unrolled, displaying a map of the Iber River, which went through Sedetani lands. Plans for the new amphitheater were on a nearby table, momentarily ignored. Standing next to the king was the commander of the army, General Hilerno alongside a dozen nobles of the Arevaci. Aristæus, the Hellenic advisor, was close by too, standing by the druid Piresso.

King Caros was a handsome man. Short dark hair framed a square jaw, which was adorned with a beard, neatly trimmed. His eyes were kind and intelligent. Though he had a white Celtic tunic trimmed in blue, over this he wore a foreign garment called a "Chlamys." The cloak was pinned at the shoulder with a brooch. A golden crown sat on his head, but it didn't stop a dark lock of hair from falling over his face. He held a gold scepter in one hand.

Piresso had an impassive face, intelligent eyes, and a long beard. He had wild dark hair that fell in curls around his shoulders. A tattoo of a stag adorned his bare chest. Aia had always valued his opinion in the past. The druid spoke to the king, "As long as the mists of doubt envelop you, be still. Wait until the sunlight burns away the fog. Then go forward with courage."

One of the officers standing near the door blocked her path. "How did you get in here?"

Eyes full of innocence, Aia shook her head. "Hmm?"

The officer glared at the doorway. "I shall have to have a talk with my men."

The king looked up and interrupted, "Never mind, captain." The king had an impatient look in his eyes as he addressed Aia. "What is it?"

Aia resisted an urge to shout. "Why have you executed Biurtan?"

King Caros looked down at the plans and replied in a distracted tone, "He and his men murdered a company of Sedetani soldiers after they wandered into our lands."

Aia nearly lost her voice. "Murdered?"

General Hilerno was a tall, muscular man with long blonde hair, a trimmed beard and a black coat of mail. He had a masterful set of features and his eyes were full of dreams. Although he had an amused expression on his face, his voice was still deep and commanding. "We are not at war with the Sedetani, Aia."

Aia shouted, "But the Lusones are our friends!" She stared into the king's eyes but he didn't look up from the map. Her voice fell like leaves out of a tree, "Biurtan was one of our best soldiers." She shook her head. "He was a fine leader."

Caros looked up, "He disobeyed my commands, Aia."

"What commands?"

Piresso answered, "Not to slay enemy soldiers if they can be captured." The druid looked into Aia's eyes. "He went—"

"Biurtan was too bloodthirsty." Caros made a conciliatory motion after interrupting the druid. "He had to be made an example of."

Aia put her hands on her hips. "Do you know where I've been the past few weeks?"

Hilerno crossed his arms. "Do tell, princess."

"I went to help the Lusones in their war against the Sedetani."

13

King Caros glared at Aia in silence, along with the nobles around the council chamber.

Hilerno looked dubious. "How is it that you have returned to us so safely?"

She had difficulty hiding her smile. "It wasn't too difficult to move about their camp. I even managed to trick the imperial guardsmen into releasing a dozen women taken as slaves."

The king was seething. "Is my daughter an honorable warrior? No. She uses deceit, enticing words and the habits of a thief. Your actions have offended the honor of our people."

Aia was taken aback. "I thought you wanted us to be clever when dealing with our enemies."

Piresso placed his hands upon the table. "A clever warrior doesn't flee from battle. You shouldn't have run away from a good fight."

Aia gazed into the druid's eyes, not comprehending his words. Feeling the weight of all eyes in the room upon her, she managed to find her voice just the same. "There was a battle at Burzao. The Sedetani destroyed the Lusones army." Her voice broke. "The next town was left completely defenseless. Turiazu has fallen."

Aristæus spoke for the first time. "That is our world: The strong and the weak. Warfare is part of life, is it not?"

Aia wondered at his remark, since he was always talking about the higher virtues. The Hellene had ice blue eyes and long blonde hair. He wore a plain white chiton bordered in purple. Aristæus was a man who liked to make plans and he expected others to fall in line with them. Aia thought him patronizing and annoying.

"They murder wounded men who lay on the field," Aia's voice turned cold, "and children."

Caros sighed audibly. "What do you want me to do, Aia?"

She looked him in the eyes. "You could speak the truth for a change. Those soldiers didn't wander into our lands. They were obviously a scouting party in preparation for an invasion." Aia remembered the words of General Orisos: *The gateway to paradise is under the shade of swords.* "Their gods are evil."

The king looked down his nose. "The Sedetani are a peaceful people."

Having come from the battlefield, Aia was incredulous. "How can you say that?"

"Yes, there's a small band of Sedetani druids who have too much influence," said the king, "but their tribe has always been dedicated to peace."

It seemed that the king's official policy was to distort the true violent nature of the Sedetani. Aia shook her head. "King Culchas is a cruel tyrant. We should send out additional war parties to protect our borders."

General Hilerno said, "Absolutely not—not for a simple patrol."

Aia glared at the general. "We need to be more aggressive when dealing with them."

Caros raised his hand to silence their argument. "An escalation of violence will go nowhere. We need to understand how they feel so that we can make peace."

Aia knew what kind of peace the Sedetani offered: Slavery and death. "You are a fool, father!"

"Would you have me become like Culchas?" asked the king. "We are not animals. Violence will always lead to more violence. That is where your path leads."

A dark hole burned in Aia's heart. "No. We shall all become subservient slaves."

"Enough!" shouted Caros. He turned to Piresso. "You are the Ard Fili, the highest judge among our people. Aia ran away from battle at Burzao. What say you?"

A shadow fell over Piresso's face. "The Honor Price is too high for such an offense. Would you cast out your own daughter?"

"Don't bother answering!" Furious, Aia stormed out of the council chamber.

The king shouted as she went out, "Go then! You are banished. Do not return to me until you've embraced a more civilized attitude. Perhaps you'll discover your honor when you do so."

Aia was shaking when she went out the door. She was banished. An outcast.

Just outside the council chamber, Hilerno caught up to her. He leaned against the wall, blocking her path. "What are you doing here? You should have been preparing for the feast. You were expected at my side tonight."

Aia looked down the hallway. Torchlight flickered across the stone, causing the shadows to dance. "Nothing has changed."

"Everything has changed."

Aia narrowed her eyes and glared at the general.

Hilerno's tone became softer. "You need to calm down, Aia," he said. "After you and I are wed, I'll get the king to agree with us. Then we can wage war on our terms."

Aia laughed in his face.

Hilerno's voice turned to ice. "You shall be mine, princess."

"Get out of my way."

* * *

Aia lay on her stomach at the water's edge, pressing her elbows into the grass. The clearing lay beneath a hush of green, the grass thick and undisturbed, glowing with the warmth of the sun. The

16

waterfall misted over the pool, hiding its secrets. A ripple underneath the calm surface betrayed the approach of a swimmer. Birds shrieked out and scattered into the sky when he burst through the water's surface, splattering water over the grassy clearing.

Aia laughed, enjoying the feel of the cold water on her legs. "Come here, Karbelos!"

A quiet voice interrupted the memory. "What are you thinking about, princess?"

Aia stood on her chamber balcony, overlooking the river. The music of flowing water rippled up to the palace, but she couldn't see the water: The sky stretched clear and cold, lit only by a fading moon. Sweet jasmine hung in the still air, but the world lay beneath a veil of shadow.

Turning around, she saw the Hellene standing in the open doorway. Bright blue eyes reflected the candlelight underneath dark eyebrows. In his arms, he carried a white linen dress, as if it were something precious. Aia looked out of the window again, peering into the darkness. "Night is returning."

Aristæus tilted his head. "I don't understand."

Aia shook her head at his ignorance. The dark half of the month began with the new moon. "All of the world's calamities come out of darkness." She looked up into the night sky. The stars shone brighter when the moon was fading. "I was thinking that we shall all perish when the Sedetani arrive. My father is too weak to resist them."

"He wants to wage a new kind of warfare—that's all." Aristæus walked into the room and placed the dress onto a table. Though he was fluent in Celtiberian, his foreign accent remained. It was a mark of pride for him. "I've brought you a gift. It's called a 'peplos.' The women of my country adorn themselves with these kinds of garments. This dress was made by Phaidra, the finest seamstress in all of Athens. The material comes from the black lands of Aígyptos far out across the sea."

Aia turned around and glanced at the dress. The material looked too light to be of any use against the elements. Her animal skins were enough. "There is no honor in this new kind of warfare, Aristæus. How can weakness win a battle?"

The Hellene chuckled. "Since your recent journey to Burzao, how can you talk of honor? After running away from battle, didn't you use deception to rescue a group of slaves?"

Aia narrowed her eyes against him but remained silent.

"Forgive me, princess. I only wish to help your people." Aristæus walked over to the balcony, gazing into the sky. "Anaximandros, who was a philosopher in my country, says that the heavens arise from a mixture of heat and cold. The stars are wheel-shaped masses of air, full of fire, breathing out flames from pores in different parts."

Aia wrinkled her nose at the high sounding words. All the Hellene offered was a life of mediocrity. She longed to return to the wilderness: Back to the lands where gods and heroes roamed. Aia crossed her arms. "There is no glory in the world you would have us live in."

"What of your world? Before I came here, your people lived in mud huts hidden behind wooden walls." Aristæus came back inside, out of the darkness. "All of your people are too fond of warfare."

"I wonder—which world is stronger?" Aia looked him in the eye. "Your world is so cold and uncaring. At least we strive for what's right."

Aristæus chuckled. "You prefer to remain in your world?"

Stepping over to the table, Aia examined the dress he'd brought as if it were a set of chains. Such a pretty thing it was. "I would have us live in a different kind of world: A place of freedom, a place of honor, a place of glory."

Aristæus held a smooth white stone in one hand, which he continually massaged with thumb and forefinger. "And what of your enemies?" he asked.

Aia put the dress down. "Why should we have any enemies?"

Aristæus grinned. "Truly, goodness is the greatest thing in the world."

Aia whispered, "The world destroys good men."

"Not always, princess," said Aristæus. "Your father is a good man."

The Arevaci had been vanquished already because they were incapable of waging warfare, but they hadn't realized it yet. Aia looked outside, into the blackness. "I have no father."

Aristæus didn't respond. The Hellene bowed politely and went out of her chamber.

Aia turned around and stepped out onto the balcony. A cool summer breeze swept over the water and into the palace. Shivering, she looked up at the River of Heaven and wondered at the stars.

A white flash lit the sky, followed by a thunderclap.

For a moment, her eyes were blinded by light.

A star ignited into an inferno, bathing the world with its brilliance. Brighter than the sun, the star came down, hurled out of the ethereal sky in resplendent fire. An arc of flame blazed across the sky to the southeast, where the star fell. Darkness spilled into the night again. There was another flash. Thunder rolled over the land and the earth shook.

Aia grabbed onto the stone railing to keep from falling to the ground.

Far out over the plains, a red glow remained. It was as if the star had opened up a fiery gulf in the earth. Aia wondered what

19

fierce contention had occurred in the heavens. Had a god fallen out of the sky?

Turning away from the distant conflagration, Aia went out of the palace in search of her horse. Tonight, she would ride into an inferno.

*   *   *

CHAPTER TWO
The Dark Queen

Aia traveled for many days with a pillar of smoke always before her. At night, she made camp in view of the distant inferno—a red glow simmering in the darkness. Arriving at the town of Araticos, the Titti people told her of the fire which had fallen out of the sky. An almighty power had cast a star out of the heavens. Now it lay burning in hideous ruin to the south, beyond the Salo River.

Aia walked through a field of wheat, leading her horse by the bridle. Though the sun was going down, she noticed a troop of horses near a farmhouse. She wondered if a Sedetani patrol had come near lands occupied by the Titti people. Shielding her eyes from the sun, she noticed soldiers wearing white tunics bordered in blue. They had a large iron plate strapped to their chests and iron greaves covering their shins. They carried small round shields, spears and curved Falcata swords. Iron helmets with cheek guards and horse hair plumes protected their heads. A few of them wore strange amulets around their necks, made from a fragment of clear crystal. They were part of the Uiroi Uiramos—*Superior Ones*—elite soldiers. She smiled. They were an Arevaci war band returning from the frontier.

As she neared the edge of the wheat field, a sentry whistled. Aia walked into a clearing near the farmhouse and stopped under a pear tree. As her horse came to a halt, she put her hand up to caress his neck. Several soldiers approached, led by a man she recognized. She called out, "Likinos!"

The captain was shorter than most of his men, but he was twice as strong as any of them. As he drew near, she inhaled a sweet fragrance: He held a pear in one hand. "Aia? What are you doing here?"

She grinned at the surprise in his face. "Curiosity," she said.

The distant fires cast a red glow over Likenos. The expression on his face turned to suspicion. "Do not meddle with the fallen star, princess." Likinos put a hand on her shoulder. "You need to get away from here."

Aia's smile went away. She didn't want anyone to call her that, now that her father had thrown her out. Her eyes swept over the plains, down to the river and across, into fire and ash. The Belli people lived there. "Tell me about the fire that came out of heaven."

"The wrath of the gods has descended upon us." He threw a glance over his shoulder at the distant inferno just before cutting the pear in two. "The fallen star struck Sekaiza."

Aia gasped in surprise. The capital city of the Belli people had been obliterated. Once a proud fortress full of tall spires, she remembered watching the city's pale yellow banners blow in the breeze last summer. All that remained of it now was a cloud of ash on the horizon. Aia whispered, "What of their people?"

22

A shadow fell over his face as he spoke. "Most of them have perished. We believe King Indortes was in the capital. Bilbiliz is on fire too, but we don't think the flames will spread across the river." He offered her half the pear. She took it but didn't take a bite. He motioned towards their camp near the farmhouse. "Come."

As they walked, Aia noticed a pair of standing stones over-looking a plain that descended to the river. The gray stones were three times the height of a man and covered with ancient writing. They stood at an angle, as if they'd borne the brunt of a gale lasting millennia. Aia tilted her head, examining the monoliths.

Likinos noticed where her eyes had wandered. "We travel by a different path, princess."

All innocence now, Aia raised her eyebrows. "It's said that those who step through the gap in those stones are changed forever. That trail leads into another world."

Aia looked at the space between the stones. The ground looked no different, except for a field of bluebells growing on either side of a path descending to the river below. "What kind of world?"

Likinos looked at the setting sun, whose light was now shining through the gap between the stones. "The land of the gods—a place for heroes," he said. He turned his back on the monoliths. "A place to die in," he murmured. "Legends say that path is haunted by the Estantigua—Dark Faeries."

Aia narrowed her eyes. "Why won't you travel along it?"

"Mortals should not meddle in the affairs of the gods." Likinos chuckled. "Besides, the Sedetani have launched an invasion. We've seen their soldiers traveling up the Salo River towards Bilbiliz." He glanced back at the burning cloud. "We must bring a report back to your father." He walked away from the firestorm, towards his camp. "Return with us."

23

The orange sky was bathed in blood. Aia couldn't take her eyes off the inferno.

Likinos halted, glancing back into the firestorm. "There is nothing there but fire and death, princess."

Aia observed the fiery glow from the sky as it spread over the field of bluebells. "There is nothing for me at home, either." She looked into his eyes. "I watched the Sedetani army destroy Turiazu. Even so, our king will not fight them."

Surprise slipped into his face. "You were among those honoring the token of friendship?"

Aia nodded her head. "The king sent only a few hundred men to fight with the Lusones. He forbade me to go." She grinned. "So I went anyway."

Likenos put his hands on his hips. "How is it that you have returned from the battle while your comrades have died with honor?"

Aia looked away, back into the firestorm across the Salo River.

"And now you think to challenge the gods?" Likenos huffed. "You're just another silly girl, aren't you?"

Ashamed, Aia didn't respond, continuing to gaze into the swirling fires across the water.

* * *

Aia lay on the grass by a small river, basking in the sunlight. The sound of a horse approached and she sat up, shading her eyes. A rider came to a stop just on the other side of the river. He was a tall man with short black hair and fair features. Smiling, he brought his horse into a gallop, aiming for the river.

Aia hugged her knees.

At the river's edge, the horse stopped suddenly, throwing the rider into the water.

Withholding laughter, Aia looked on as the man, cursing,

struggled out of the river.

The white horse—the noblest creature she'd ever seen—whinnied, as if he was laughing at the man. The horse walked down into the river, waded across, passed the man and climbed out of the water.

The man glared at his mount, "Very funny."

Aia stood up to greet the horse. She called out, "He swims better than you do."

Bare-chested, the man wore leather pants and boots. The shadow of a beard gave him a noble appearance and he had kind, intelligent brown eyes. A gold medallion on a leather cord encircled his neck. "He wasn't thrown in."

"He wasn't trying to impress anyone, either." Aia looked into his eyes and felt her heart race.

The man remained silent, gazing deeply into her eyes.

After a moment she found her tongue. "What brings you to Arcailicos?"

The man shook himself, as if waking from a dream. He stepped over to the horse and placed his hand on the neck, taking the reins. The horse whinnied. "My father is here to visit King Caros."

Aia raised her eyebrows. "Who is your father?"

"King Olónico."

Aia smiled. "So you're a prince."

"Yes."

A shout came from across the river, "Karbelos!"

The man turned to look at the newcomer, who was seated on the back of a brown stallion. "I'm coming!" He handed the reins to Aia. "Keep him."

Aia dropped the reins. "No!"

"I have another horse." Karbelos smiled. "Besides, he seems to

25

like you."

Before she could answer, he waded back into the river, crossed it and leapt up onto the horse, behind his friend. Waving, they rode away.

Aia watched them ride up the road to the palace, unable to look away.

The white horse began to push her towards the water.

Aia waved the horse away, but once again, he nudged her forward with his nose.

She giggled. "Hey!"

Someone shook her.

Aia awoke, peering into a field of stars.

A dark figure kneeled over her, whispering, "Wake up, princess!"

One hand on a short sword, she sat up. Several figures moved through the darkness.

There was a shout.

A clash of arms came from the clearing near a bonfire. Men were killing one another.

Aia and her companion crept near the sounds and stopped under the pear tree. They could see men fighting in the flickering light. She tried to make out who the combatants were, but they were all dressed alike.

Several shadowy figures strode into view, brandishing swords and spears. One threw a spear, impaling her companion. Another man rushed forward aiming a blow at Aia's head.

Aia ducked the sword strike and stabbed the soldier with her short sword. She leapt into the fray, striking down a man and ducking under another blade.

Two men ran towards her, striking together.

Aia tumbled out of the way of both of their swords and stood up to face them.

This time, one leapt out before his companion.

Aia struck down at his helmet, cracking it. He fell without uttering a sound.

The second man moved forward, swinging several blows as he came on.

She retreated back out of the firelight.

Her opponent overextended himself and she struck him down.

Someone hit her in the back and Aia fell to the ground. A man holding a sword and shield leaned down, glaring at her. She noticed that he was one of their soldiers. Firelight flickered off the clear crystal hanging down on a leather cord. On impulse, she grabbed the amulet and yanked it from his neck.

The man froze in his tracks. A whisper of despair emptied into the darkness while luminous vapor seeped out of his head. He shook all over, as if all of the warmth in his body was bleeding into the sky.

Rolling out from under her assailant, she stood up.

The man had a blank expression on his face. He shook his head and looked over his shoulder into the firelight. As his gaze returned, his expression changed to confusion.

Aia glanced down at the amulet. Striations of silver and gold were embedded within the stone and red firelight flickered off its surface. Cold whispers emanated from the crystal, sending a chill down her spine. Dropping the stone, she shouted into the fray, "Take their amulets away! They're under an enchantment!"

Someone knocked her to the ground.

Rolling over, she saw Likenos standing over her, sword in hand.

He brought his sword down toward her head.

Rolling out of the way, she used her legs to trip him.

A moment later, she was on top of him.

Before he could strike her, she grabbed the amulet and yanked it away from his neck. Like a candle blown out, the fierce expression in his eyes was extinguished.

"Tell me," she said, rolling off him, "where did you get these charms?"

He blinked as life returned to his eyes. "There was a woman on the side of the road just outside of Nertobis, selling potions and charms." Likenos sat up onto his elbows. "She said these crystal amulets would protect us against evil spirits."

"What did she call herself?"

"Lilura."

Aia closed her hand around the crystal, balling it into a fist. "I shall remember your name, Lilura."

* * *

Unable to reveal that she'd been banished, Aia refused to return home with the scouting party. They rode away, singing. As she watched them go, all of the warmth in her heart faded away. Was she truly a warrior without honor? She shook her head, dismissing them. The thought of traveling with such brave men was unbearable anyway. She turned her gaze south, to the distant firestorm.

While walking around the monoliths, Aia put out a hand and ran it along cool stone, feeling the deep grooves where ancient inscriptions made a mark. Though she couldn't read the words, she wondered if the Tartessians had carved them after escaping from Atlantis. Did the pair of stones mark the boundary to another world—just as Likenos had said?

Getting on her horse, she circled around them once more and placed herself in front of the monoliths. The sun rose out of the distant mountains, pierced the veil of smoke and threw a red light over the bluebells. When the light touched the center of the trail, she kicked her horse into a gallop, riding downhill through the gap in the stones.

She felt something, like a whisper, caress her skin as she rode between the stones. The light dimmed slightly and she wondered if the distant cloud of ash had blackened the sun. Shrugging, Aia descended along the path through bluebells, feeling as if someone was observing her movements.

Riding downhill towards the Salo River took all day. As the sun was going down, she came to a grove of almond trees lined up like a company of soldiers standing to attention. A hot gale blew through the trees. Aia looked up at the fuzzy green almond hulls hanging from the branches. Beyond the trees, she could still see the red glow from the inferno on the other side of the river.

"Good evening." This came from a musical voice to the right.

The almond tree next to the path had a girl tied up to it. Clad entirely in black leather, she had long brown hair, draped over one shoulder. With a thin face and warm brown eyes, she looked completely calm, as if she was waiting for a lover to arrive for a tryst in the forest. A prominent bouquet of bluebells lay at her feet, discarded.

Aia held back a smile as she scanned the road. "Yes, it is."

The girl went on in a friendly tone. "You seem to be going in the wrong direction."

Aia shrugged, running a hand along the mane of her horse. "I like the south."

The girl's voice held a distinctive accent. "Perhaps you could do me a favor before you continue on to your fiery death."

Looking down at the gray strands of rope binding the girl to the tree, Aia wondered what they were made from. "You want a knife."

29

"Actually, no," whispered the girl in a conspiratorial tone. "I wonder if you could scratch my nose. It's been tickling me for quite some time."

Aia noticed a little ball of light far off down the path. It whisked off into the forest, as if it wanted to remain hidden. "I'd rather not get off my horse." She glanced up into the trees. "It's getting dark."

"Yes of course," grumbled the girl. "What's your name?"

"Aia."

"A pleasure," said the girl. "I'm Nescato."

For an instant Aia considered releasing the girl, but she didn't want to antagonize those who'd tied her up. Holding back an urge to ride on, Aia gave way to curiosity. "What's an Aquitanian doing so far south?"

Nescato's smile was a shy one. "How is it you know where I'm from?"

Aia sat up in her saddle, making ready to leave. "You have an accent."

Taking note of Aia's imminent departure, Nescato raised her voice. "I was in Bilbiliz when the fire came out of the sky. All of the bridges across the Salo River have been burnt."

"How did you get across?"

Nescato smiled. "I found a boat. I can take you there if you want."

Aia wondered who'd tied up the girl. "I thought you were going the other way."

"I'm not going anywhere at the moment."

Taking out a knife, Aia tossed it down. It stuck into the tree next to Nescato's hand.

Far down the trail, another flicker of light appeared. Aia peered ahead, trying to make out who it might be. More lights appeared behind the first one, forming a long procession. A line of tall figures approached, carrying candles.

Without warning, Nescato uttered a shrill cry.

All of the color in Nescato's face had drained away. She was staring at something on the other side of the path. Aia drew her long sword from the sheath on her back but her horse reared up, throwing her to the ground. The sword clattered away into the dark. Whinnying in terror, her horse galloped off into the night.

A sighing sound emanated out of the blackness. Aia felt the hair on the back of her neck stand up. The tormented whisper turned into a girl's voice, cold and dismal, as if she'd spent an eternity alone in darkness. The words were in the ancient Tartessian language.

"What a pretty bouquet of bluebells."

Aia glanced at Nescato, but she couldn't see her face any longer. Getting up, Aia drew her short sword. Peering into the night, she could make out the luminous outline of a girl, holding a rag doll in one hand. Her eyes were as empty as the surrounding darkness. The girl turned her gaze towards Aia.

Aia felt a chill run down her spine. She tightened the grip on her sword.

Floating across the ground, the girl swept forward.

Aia slashed out with the sword but it met with no resistance, sliding through the girl's body like wind through the trees.

With one swift motion, the girl knocked Aia to the ground, straddling her. Icy hands gripped Aia by the throat. The cold seeped into her bones.

The girl giggled and tightened her grip. "Why do you resist?"

Aia dropped the sword, choking.

The sound of a chariot came out of the darkness.

Aia struggled, unable to breathe beneath the grip of steel.

Nescato shouted, "Stop! You've come for me, not her!"

The grip tightened. "I want you both."

A silver chariot drawn by a pair of black stallions approached, carrying a woman, pale of face, with sharp eyes. A crown of gazania and lantana wildflowers circled her head and she wore a black gown with moonstones woven into the fabric. A crude medallion made from a piece of black crystal hung from a silver chain around her neck. In an imperious tone, she spoke in the Tartessian tongue, "Release her."

The icy grip slipped away into the darkness, along with the spirit-girl, whimpering.

Aia sat up with a hand to her throat, gasping for breath.

The woman waited for Aia to recover.

Aia noticed that she was surrounded by a company of dark faeries holding candles. Grim-faced, they wore black armor and were armed with spears and swords made from silvery metal. They were all adorned with wildflowers.

Aia got to her feet.

The woman glared down from the chariot, speaking in Celtiberian this time. "Explain yourself."

Coughing to clear her throat, Aia straightened up. Inhaling a lungful of the warm night air, she bowed her head. "I'm simply a traveler."

"I would have your name."

"Aia."

"I am Faiatura, Queen of the Estantigua." She stepped down from the chariot, glancing over one shoulder. The fire cast an infernal glow over the tops of the almond grove. "Where are you bound?"

"I'm going south, Your Grace."

Faiatura tilted her head slightly, as if she were listening to whispers on the wind. She took hold of the medallion around her neck. "A dreary plain—forlorn and wild—lies beyond the river. A land of desolation, it is void of life, full of seething flames and elemental spirits. You go to your death."

A tall faerie approached the chariot, offering up both of Aia's swords. The queen took one of the blades, examining it. "How is it that you come by swords made in Toletum?"

"My people trade with the Carpetani for their steel."

The queen cast her eyes over to Nescato. The gray ropes had been cut. The girl stood next to the tree, trembling. "Why do you aid one sacrificed to us?"

Aia glanced down the trail. It teemed with dark figures, their weapons glinting in the candlelight. "I had no intention of helping her, Your Grace. I was just about to continue on with my journey when you arrived."

Pulling Aia's knife from the tree where Nescato had been bound, a Faerie brought it over. The queen's smile turned cold. "It seems that you've forgotten one of your weapons."

Aia bit her lip.

Faiatura handed the knife over to one in her retinue, who gave it to Aia. The Dark Queen glanced at Nescato. "Is she of value?"

With a sigh, Aia shrugged and said, "I wouldn't really know, Your Grace."

Mirth slipped into the queen's eyes. "You're quite polite for one doomed to die."

A trio of blue lights, each no more than an inch in diameter, flew up to the queen. They brought up Aia's white horse, tethered on a silver chain. Faiatura looked at the horse with appreciation. "I shall take your horse in exchange for your lives."

Furious, Aia made a move to retrieve her horse.

33

One of the faeries intervened, thrusting his spear at Aia.

Aia moved towards the spear thrust, tricking him into maintaining his commitment to the thrust. At the last moment, she faked moving to one side, sliding forward in the opposite direction. Deflecting the spear with one hand, she grabbed the spear and moved up the weapon, hand-over-hand fashion until she reached her adversary. Striking him in the throat, he went down and she took the spear out of his hands. Another tall figure advanced but she kicked him in the chest, knocking him to the ground. Aia spun around in a circle, twirling the spear while the rest of the Estantigua stepped back.

The faerie standing next to the queen raised a black bow, withdrew an arrow from his quiver, nocked it and pointed it at Aia. The queen raised a hand. "No. Do not kill them."

Rising out of the fighting stance, Aia glowered at the dark faeries.

The imperious eyes of the queen fixated on Aia. "Then we have a bargain."

Defeated, Aia nodded her head and threw the spear onto the ground.

A tearful Nescato leapt forward, grabbing the queen in a hug. "Thank you, Your Majesty."

Dark faeries bound Aia's horse to the queen's chariot. Faiatura got in while the rest of the Estantigua formed a procession. The queen cast a final glance in Aia's direction and said, "Go forth to your fates, but travel in daylight, for the night belongs to me."

The Estantigua rode on into the fading light.

When Aia retrieved her weapons, she considered going after them.

Nescato tugged at Aia's elbow. "Come on, we'd better get away from here."

Spinning around, Aia placed a sword at Nescato's throat. "Why should I permit you to live?"

Nescato stepped back, bewildered.

Aia pointed her sword at Nescato. "Tell me."

"I saved your life."

"No, you didn't."

"I did! I told that spirit to leave you alone."

"I don't recall her listening to you."

Nescato shouted, "It was only a horse!"

Aia lowered the sword. "I would trade your life and many others for that horse."

"Go ahead then," said Nescato. "Kill me."

Aia put her sword away and walked off down the trail towards the river. It would have been dishonorable to kill the girl. Her eyes drifted up into the glowing sky. The fallen star had ignited the world's fury into a firestorm.

* * *

Night had come. A hot wind blew in from the south where the fires burned. The red glow from the inferno illuminated a layer of ash covering the ground. At the end of the trail, Aia found another pair of standing stones, much like the ones she'd passed through near the farmhouse. They stood at the edge of a plain covered with Iberian wildflowers that swept down the slope towards the Salo River. Aia approached the end of the trail and placed a hand on one monolith, peering across the water.

Nescato crept up to the end of the path and halted by the other stone.

Aia turned inquisitive eyes towards her.

Nescato returned the gaze. "What?"

35

"Where is it?"

Biting her lip, Nescato glanced around in the direction of the river. "It was here this morning. I can't—"

"There was never any boat, was there?"

"What? Of course there was," protested Nescato.

The firelight glinted off a black crystal medallion hanging from a silver chain around the girl's neck. Nescato, noticing Aia's attention, reached up to touch it, a sly grin on her face.

"You know, the Dark Queen will come for that," warned Aia. "You should leave it here."

"That's the worst suggestion I've heard all day," murmured Nescato in a distracted tone.

Sighing, Aia shook her head. She pointed downstream, to the left. "Nertobis is that way, if you care to go." The city belonged to the Belli. Aia wondered how many of their towns had been destroyed tonight. Nertobis was most likely teeming with refugees. "Perhaps the Estantigua won't find you there."

Looking rather like a caged animal, Nescato hesitated. "Where are you going?"

Aia turned her gaze to the firestorm across the river.

Nescato tilted her head slightly. "Why is it that you want to die so desperately?"

Ignoring the girl's question, Aia walked out onto the slope, heading down to the water. Dancing flames reflected off the surface. Aia noticed figures of men silhouetted against the light. She looked up across the river and saw a column of soldiers marching towards the firestorm. Incredulity slipped into her face.

After a few minutes, Nescato ran up, grumbling to herself in Aquitanian.

Though Aia wasn't fluent in the northern tongue, she recognized a few of the words: "Basajaun, please protect me."

At the sight of the soldiers across the river, Nescato came to a stop.

A horn sounded and the column changed formation into a line. While they continued to approach the fires, the men in front brought their shields up. At the sound of another horn, the soldiers halted. The front ranks lowered their spears.

"I've got to see this." Aia ran to the edge of the river and dove in, swimming under the surface for a long while until she came up for air. She heard Nescato swimming behind but didn't stop until she had reached the far side.

A whirlwind of flame swept over the land, incinerating everything in its path. Aia stood next to the river gazing into the inferno. Nescato came up beside her, dripping wet. "Perhaps we should light a fire," she said, glancing down at her drenched clothes.

Not bothering to laugh at the joke, Aia wondered what the soldiers would do.

The contingent of Sedetani warriors wore red tunics and scale armor, and had iron helmets with a high pointed tip. Their oval shields were painted red and black and were decorated with the images of their gods. Intent on the flames, they didn't notice the two observers down by the river.

"Your curiosity is going to get me killed," grumbled Nescato.

"You don't have to follow me."

Nescato smiled. "Yes I do."

A sunburst blazed forth and a flaming chariot emerged from the firestorm, drawn by a pair of white horses. The driver's slender form was outlined against the light. Fire did not seem to harm him, though smoke seeped off his white tunic. He wore an iron helmet with cheek guards and he carried a Falcata sword. The chariot was painted white and decorated with gold. A quiver of javelins was attached to the side where a man might stand next to the driver, but no warrior rode behind him in the chariot.

The company of Sedetani soldiers seemed to draw back in apprehension at the sight of the chariot. Spirits of fire, in the shape of winged serpents emerged from the inferno, flying behind the chariot. Some of the soldiers broke ranks and ran away. The driver began to throw javelins at the soldiers, swerving the chariot around and out of range of their thrown spears. All the while, the winged serpents, wreathed in fire, attacked.

After a few minutes the company had been reduced to a handful of men. Some of the men made a final desperate attack but they couldn't catch the chariot. The rest ran away down the road. Riding down to the river's edge, the exhausted driver stumbled out of the chariot and fell forward, face down into the water while the fiery serpents flew back into the inferno.

"Come on!" Aia ran towards the man, followed by Nescato. Though he was drowning, firelight shimmered from his body, as if he were made of flame. Each taking him under arm, they carried the man out of the water.

Aia would never forget her first sight of Tekos. His tawny eyes were full of slumbering fire, but he possessed an intense power of stillness in them too. At the same time, he gave off the impression of a wild untamed animal trapped in an exquisitely carved body. His eyes lit up at the sight of Aia, as if he recognized her.

Aia waited for him to finish coughing up water before she spoke. "Why did you come down to the river?"

"I was thirsty." He raised a hand up to wipe the water off his forehead. "I touched the river and all of my strength failed me. The goddess Salo is angry with me."

38

Firelight still shimmered off his body. Aia glanced over at his chariot. The horses were drinking from the river. Their backs were smoking. "My name is Aia. This is Nescato."

"I am Tekos."

"Why were you battling the Sedetani?"

"They have invaded our lands."

Nescato looked concerned. "Has Nertobis fallen?"

"No, but they travel on the south side of the river to avoid a fight." As if he were a burning coal whose fire had finally gone out, the light faded away from Tekos. He stood up. "My companion, Baisebilos and I were returning to the capital from Orosiz when the star fell out of the sky."

Nescato glanced around. "Your companion?"

"Last night," said Tekos, "he fell in battle."

Aia's voice dropped to a whisper. "You saw where the star landed?"

Tekos gave her an intense look. "Yes."

"Can you take me there?"

He shook his head. "I will stay here to defend this road."

Aia put a hand on his shoulder. "Tekos, your people are gone. King Indortes is dead."

"He may still be alive."

Aia looked at the wall of fire. "How could he have survived that?"

Tekos turned away to face the river, barren. A hot wind blew through the valley, carrying burning embers along with it. The sound of running water washed away the firestorm at their backs. Tekos seemed to come to a decision. "You saved my life. On my honor I will serve you both until the end of my days."

A smile touched Aia's lips. "Just take me to the place where the star landed."

Nescato jumped into the conversation. "We're glad to accept your service, Tekos." Turning an annoyed expression towards Aia, she motioned towards the chariot.

"Perhaps you should tend to your horses," said Aia. "Tomorrow we can begin our journey."

Tekos moved off into the firelight.

Nescato put her arm around Aia.

"Don't ruin a good thing," she whispered. "How did you know he was fighting the Sedetani?"

"They fight in close formations like their allies, the Carthaginians." Aia looked into the inferno, wondering how Tekos had managed to pass through the fire.

"The Carthaginians have other allies, Aia."

She saw again the dead, heaped in piled before the gates of Turiazu. "I've seen them fight before."

Perhaps sensing a change in Aia's mood, Nescato changed the subject. "Why do you want to go where the star fell to the earth?"

Aia whispered, "Because glory is only bestowed upon those who seek it."

*   *   *

CHAPTER THREE
The Pit

Aia gazed into a wall of fury, wishing that it would burn away her unworthiness. A swift breeze washed over her back, reminding her of summers past where her father used to take her riding past tall trees that protected the vineyards from storms. No trees would offer any protection now. The destruction of the Celtiberians approached like a wall of flame. One by one their kingdoms would fall—another tree caught up in the conflagration. Their destiny was not to fight—they were doomed to fall and be forgotten. Good men like her father had no place in this world. Without the chance to seek honor and glory in battle, Aia would face a life of mediocrity and shame if she remained at home. Better to face the wall of fire.

Aia sat in front of Nescato while the girl finished braiding Aia's hair. Peering into the flames, Aia thought she could see spirits dancing there.

A soft whisper rose from the crackling fire, "Come to me."

A moment later, the wind picked up, covering the whispers and carrying the bright faces away into the coming dawn.

Nescato's voice intruded. "You think we can capture the fallen star?"

Aia smiled. "We?"

"Do you really think I'd let you keep Tekos all for yourself?" Nescato's voice quivered. "Though the idea of riding into that—" Nescato's hands grew still. She stood up. "Come on, we'd better go find out where our driver has got to."

"He's retrieving his javelins," said Aia.

While they waited, they tied damp cloths around their faces, soaked their braided hair and wrapped themselves in wet blankets. Again, Aia wondered how Tekos and his team of horses had passed through the fire without harm.

Tekos emerged from behind a hill, carrying a dozen javelins he had gathered from the field. As he inserted them in the quiver inside the chariot, he looked up at the horizon where the star had come down. Beyond the wall of fire, a column of smoke ascended into the morning sky. "Do you think it's wise, seeking the fallen star? Death surrounds it. Perhaps it is not meant to be disturbed."

"Nonsense," said Aia as she got into the chariot. "Shall we go?"

With a shrug Tekos stepped into the driver's position in front of Aia. As Nescato climbed in, Aia heard her say aloud, "I wonder what kind of jewel it was that burned so brightly in heaven?"

Tekos grumbled, "A god has been cast out of the sky and she talks of trinkets."

Passing through the firestorm was like diving into a cool lake on a summer's day. Aia could feel a chilly wave wash over her when they entered the wall of fire. Though she had instinctively closed her eyes at the threshold of the barrier, she opened them again, surprised at the strange sensation. Scattered sunshine emanated from Tekos, his team of horses and the chariot itself. Aia held up her hand and found that it too, shone with sunlight. Inhaling deeply, she breathed in icy clear air and shivered. No trace of smoke or ash touched her nose.

Nescato stood up and lowered her face mask to whisper in Aia's ear. "The supreme goddess Mari has granted us protection during our journey through the fire."

Aia laughed. "More likely it's Trebaruna. The war goddess is always fond of heroes."

Tekos called back over his shoulder. "Nay, the fallen star is watching. It calls to us. I have long felt it drawing me thither."

They rode through a barren land full of ash. Small flames burned here and there still, consuming the final traces of life. The Belli tribes had inhabited the land only a few days ago, but now all of the hills were black ash. They came to a place where all of the trees had been blasted flat. On one side of the blasted area, a grove of plum trees had once grown. Tekos paused to look down a road. It descended into a valley to the right of the blasted plain.

Aia turned her gaze away from the column of smoke up ahead. She looked down the road. "Why have you stopped?"

Tekos turned around to face them. "This road leads to Sekaiza, the capital city of the Belli. The star has annihilated my people. Why do you want to go to the seat of desolation?"

Aia looked into his calm eyes. "My people, the Arevaci, are facing destruction too, from the Sedetani invaders."

Tekos looked doubtful. "The Arevaci are the most powerful tribe in all of Celtiberia. Will they not fight?"

"No."

"Then how will a fallen star help you?"

43

Aia smiled. "A flower falling from the gardens of heaven will always smell sweet."

Tekos shrugged and pointed toward the hill up ahead, directly under the column of smoke. "There is your star. It lies vanquished, at the bottom of a fiery pit."

"Will you not approach?"

Tekos shook his head.

"Why not?"

Tekos whispered, "Because it calls to me."

Aia nodded, "Very well."

"I shall remain here," he pointed at a burned-out house beside the incinerated grove of plumb trees, "until you return."

Aia stepped off the chariot and glanced at Nescato, who remained where she was. Aia saw that the girl was trembling.

Nescato shrugged. "Perhaps the jewel of heaven no longer burns so brightly."

"What happened to your curiosity?"

Nescato looked down. "I suppose I'm not as eager as you are."

Taking an extra leather water bottle, Aia turned her back on the two, drawn forward by promises whispering on the wind. Visions mingled with the rustling voice like sunlight shining on a field of flowers. Aia imagined a life surrounded by gold and jewels and a life of honor among her people. The dreams were intoxicating.

The summer heat rippled into the sky and mingled with the column of smoke coming from just over the hill. Taking a moment to rest before climbing up to the crest, Aia wiped the sweat off her brow. A gust of wind called out, drawing her forward. Dropping an empty water bottle, Aia made her way to the top.

A tremendous pit lay before her, fuming. Small fires still burned in places. The walls of the pit were nearly vertical, making any descent hazardous. Aia peered across the gulf, wondering if an arrow could reach the other side, but it was entirely obscured by smoke. Down inside the pit something stirred at the core behind the tower of rising smoke.

Aia remained where she was, listening. No voice came out of the fire or whispered over the wind. She looked into the sky. Did the gods fight among the stars?

Aia's descent took more than an hour. As she made her way to the center of the pit, the found the ground littered with footprints. Near the excavation site, a mound of earth had been piled. Wheel marks led off toward the far side, and for the first time, Aia notice a narrow ledge carved into the pit wall. Cursing, she headed toward the road that led up and out.

During her ascent, a frightful cheer shattered the silence. It rose again and again, each echo sending a cold chill down her spine. At last there came a dreadful silence. She had to force herself to continue on, curiosity getting the better of her fears.

Voices drifted by as she emerged from the pit.

"Tell Tyresius not to accept any gifts from the fallen god."

Laughter preceded the response. "Yes, Lord Culchas."

Sounds of retreating horses marked a cavalcade marching away.

Aia stepped out onto a field filled with Sedetani soldiers standing at attention. Sunlight glinted off spear tips and gleamed on iron helmets. Colorful banners flew overhead. A line of chariots stood before the soldiers, alongside several riders on horseback.

Aia recognized King Culchas and General Orisos. Culchas held a bloody sword in one hand and stood atop a makeshift wooden platform before a contingent of soldiers. He was covered in blood.

Nearby, the bodies of several men and women lay in a heap. In the distance, a covered wagon trundled away, escorted by a hundred men.

One of the riders was a pretty young woman with melancholy eyes. Long brown hair fell straight down her back. Some violent emotion seemed to be mastering her. She was the first person to notice the intruder, though she said nothing.

After a moment, a soldier shouted an alarm. Aia was surrounded by a ring of spears and had to surrender. Rough hands dragged her forward and she was thrown at the feet of the king. Culchas glared down at her with eyes of steel. Rising off the barren earth, Aia wiped ash off her face, and glared back at the king of the Sedetani. A soldier kicked her in the side, knocking her down.

Aia rose again, defiant.

General Orisos asked, "What is your name, girl?"

"My name is Aia, of the Arevaci."

A horse stepped forward. Aia looked on with curiosity at the rider. He had an alien air about him. Clad in robes of white and purple, he held a black stone in one hand, endlessly rubbing it between thumb and forefinger. With a pale face and washed-out blonde hair, the man had a curious, unsettling impassivity. Despite this, his voice was deep and pleasant.

"What are you doing here?"

The foreigner had such a strange look about him that Aia was too distracted to respond.

"This is none of your concern, Baalhaan," Orisos said. "Kill her."

A knife came up to Aia's throat.

Culchas raised his hand. "Wait."

Aia no longer felt the knife.

Culchas leaned forward. "I've seen you somewhere."

His hard eyes drew Aia back to the present. "That can't be true,"

46

she said with a grin, "I was never there."

Culchas laughed. "That's right—you lay on the battlefield at Burzao, one of the dead. So you were pretending?" He looked at his general. "Don't you recognize her, Orisos?"

"This one is trouble." Orisos grumbled. "We should kill her."

"One such as this isn't worth killing," said Culchas. "Thieves have no honor."

Aia felt a wave of shame wash over her, to mingle with the hot sun.

Culchas drew her eyes into his with a fierce look. "Why have you come here?"

"I was hiding from soldiers out of Arcobis." Aia glanced at the horizon to give credence to her lie. "An army approaches from the west." She smiled. "I didn't want to be out in the open when they come over that hill."

While none of the soldiers at attention showed any signs of a reaction, some of the king's men on horses looked nervous. General Orisos directed his gaze at Culchas who, unconvinced, hadn't taken his eyes off of his captive.

Aia considered the pit and shrugged. "I wanted to see the fallen star."

Culchas glanced at the departing wagon. "The fallen god serves me now." A cruel smile slipped across his face. "The Belli people have been extinguished." He looked toward the horizon. "Now, every knee will bend before me and every tongue shall give glory to my greatness."

Aia narrowed her eyes. "You will never be great."

"Why do you say that?"

"Because you are not a good man," she whispered.

"I am a strong man."

Aia stood in the blazing sun, wondering if Culchas would turn the world to ash.

"Release her," he commanded.

The steel grip on her arms went away.

The foreigner Baalhaan said, "Take her with us, Lord Culchas. I can make a fortune selling her as a slave."

Culchas chuckled. "Carthaginians are the greediest bastards I've ever encountered." Shaking his head, Culchas took up a cloth and wiped the blood off his sword. "No, I have another use for this one."

An ornate box was placed before Aia. Culchas made a motion and Orisos shouted a command to the contingent of soldiers, who began marching away to the east. Culchas gave Aia one final look before riding away in his chariot. "A gift for the King of the Arevaci," he said. "Tell Caros the Sedetani are coming."

Aia watched them move away from the setting sun until they sank below the hill, trampling ash into the earth.

* * *

Tekos brought the chariot to a halt. "This is the first time I've traveled north of the Salo River. What is this place?"

Aia pointed at the mountain fortress standing before them. It had a clear view of all the lands to the south. Three peaks cast their shadows over the stronghold. "We call these mountains 'The Three Mothers,'" she said. "Beyond are the conquered cities of Belsinon, Burzao and Turiazu." Aia grew silent. It was where her life had come to an end.

"Not very high mountains, are they?" Nescato stood up to look at the fortress standing on a high bluff at the foot of the mountain. The fading sunlight turned the walls to fire. "Why have we come here?"

"Because you didn't want us to leave you at Nertobis," said Aia.

"Too many have come to that city," grumbled Nescato. "Its streets are full of desperate people now."

Tekos chuckled. "The ideal place for one endowed with your unique talents."

"That's not a nice thing to say," pouted Nescato. "Not a nice thing to say at all."

Aia looked up at the fortress. "This is the city of Titum, where King Situbolai lives. His people are the Titti tribesmen who dwell in the hills on the north side of the Salo River. Its walls are guarded with magic and its gates are protected by wards of power. They say this city will never fall to an invader while the king lives."

"I know all that," moaned Nescato. "Why have we come here?"

"I will ask the king to help me capture the fallen god."

Nescato sat down in the chariot. "He won't see you."

Aia looked down at the chest next to her feet. "He will."

Though Tekos was obviously curious, he didn't ask what Aia had brought back from the pit. He looked at the chest muttering to himself, "Fire and ash for a king."

Leaving the others to find lodging in the lower city, Aia went up to the citadel, carrying the small chest. The road cut between two hills faced in stone and topped with wooden walls. Wooden guard towers watched over the plains that went down into the Salo River valley. Walking towards the gate to the fortress, she heard a voice. "Princess Aia!"

Wearing the white uniform of a company commander from the Arevaci town of Termesos, a man carrying a spear approached. With long blonde hair and blue eyes, Aia could never resist flirting with the man whenever she'd seen him. Halting by a low stone bridge leading over a mountain stream that ran through the city, Aia placed the box on the ground and ran a hand through her hair.

"Hello, Urcaildu."

The sound of running water tumbled over his words. "Are you here for the libation rituals tonight?"

"Of course," she lied. Aia had no idea what he was talking about. Realizing that her father was here to visit the king of the Titti people, Aia wondered if she could get King Situbolai to help her.

Urcaildu rubbed his chin. "I hope the Nameless One will accept our sacrifice tonight. We brought a prize bull."

"Why would our sacrifice be rejected?"

Urcaildu threw a furtive glance at the fortress. "Piresso has been cast out."

The druid was the high priest of the Arevaci. Aia was stunned. "Why?"

"His words were considered offensive to the Sedetani. One of the priests of Neito traveling through Arcailicos demanded that our king remove all those who speak words distasteful to the Sedetani."

"What words did he give?"

Urcaildu raised his hands. "It is not permitted to speak openly about this, princess."

Aia forgot about King Situbolai for the moment. "What?"

"Many people have been imprisoned for speaking out against the Sedetani."

Aia was astonished. "They're concealing the savagery of the Sedetani from our people?" The heat of the setting sun washed over the bridge. "The king needs to accept acts of brutality for what they are."

"It's more serious than that, princess." His voice grew hot. "A dozen of my men are sitting in prison for defending our lands. They've been accused of murder."

Aia was too stunned to respond. Her father had gone mad.

Shadows grew as the sun went down, throwing blood into the streets. She hoped the insanity hadn't spread to the Titti people. Even a stronghold as secure as Titum would fall if they refused to fight. "Do you think I could get in to see King Situbolai?"

His anger abated by the distraction, Urcaildu picked up the chest at her feet. "I'll take you to him."

The stronghold's walls encircling the city were unassailable from the valley below. Nevertheless, passing along the narrow city streets, they walked through several gatehouses full of wary soldiers. It was as if the Titti people expected an attack from within. Companies of Arevaci soldiers were there too, but only Titti warriors were allowed inside the innermost wall. As they climbed the steps to the citadel, Aia heard the splash of water from a mountain stream that tumbled down alongside the steps.

Inside, they stopped at a pair of sturdy oak doors bound with iron, flanked by a pair of proud warriors. They wore green tunics and sandals that laced up their checkered breeches. Iron helmets with cheek guards and horse hair plumes rested on their heads. They were armed with spears, Falcata swords and oval shields painted in green and decorated with Celtic knotwork. The one who spoke was the taller of the two. "State your purpose in coming here."

Urcaildu put down the box, resting for a moment before he spoke. "I've brought Princess Aia to visit King Situbolai."

The warrior turned a critical eye towards Aia. "You're the one who ran away from battle at Burzao?" He shook his head. "Your honor must be intact if you want to enter these halls."

Growing hot, Aia resisted an urge to shout at the man. "I fought hard at Burzao."

"Then how did you survive?"

Urcaildu interjected, "Is King Caros here?"

The warrior held Aia's gaze for a moment before turning to respond. "Yes. They are both inside the council chamber."

"I'd like to see my father," demanded Aia.

For a second, Aia thought the guard would refuse them. The warrior seemed to relax and with a smirk on his face, he waved them in. Urcaildu picked up the chest and followed Aia through the doors.

Smoke ascended from a fire pit in the center of the large circular room. Oil burned from lamps hanging from wood beams, filling the chamber with flickering light.

Along the side of the room was a large table, surrounded by several men. A miniature landscape covered the table, made out of earth, wood and stone. It was a map displaying all of Celtiberia. Aia recognized her home Arcailicos on the Dubro River, the peaks of The Three Mothers, the Iber River Valley beyond the mountains, and the Salo River Valley to the south. The map was covered with iron figurines that moved on their own accord, as if unseen spirits were propelling them. Small soldiers marched up the Iber River Valley. A regal figurine with a crown of gold lay on its side by Turiazu, the capital city of the Lusones. The Belli capital of Sekaiza was a smoking pit. Little soldiers, chariots, and cavalry pranced across the table while miniature ships swam up and down the rivers. The magic map transformed the war into an intricate dance.

A man with white hair and a long beard held a golden scepter in one hand, which he used to point out features on the map to the others. A golden crown adorned with gems sat on his head. A pair of warriors stood by, alert. On the other side of the table stood her father, King Caros, next to Aristæus and General Hilerno. Several other advisors stood around the table.

Caros was dictating a letter to a scribe, "King Culchas, I humbly beseech you to forgive us for sending merchant ships down the Iber River without your permission. The sinking of our vessel by your warship was entirely our fault. I hope our two peoples will enjoy a lasting peace in the years to come." He waited for the scribe to catch up before he said, "Sign the letter, Caros, King of the Arevaci."

Hearing her father's words filled Aia with disgust.

Urcaildu placed the chest on the floor. Aia thanked him and gave him a hug. When Hilerno threw her an angry look, she kissed Urcaildu in defiance, bringing a smile to the warrior's lips. Hilerno stood silently by, simmering.

King Situbolai looked up. "Who are you?"

Aia stated her name and bowed.

Situbolai stepped back from the enchanted map. "We're busy at the moment, princess, but if you'd like to see your father —"

"No, Your Majesty, I've come to see you."

The two sovereigns exchanged glances. Caros said, "Where have you been, Aia?"

After their last conversation, Aia was surprised her father spoke to her. "I went to find the fallen star. It lay at the bottom of a burning pit. I met Culchas there. The fallen god serves him now. He's taken it away."

They had a look of astonishment on their faces. After a moment of silence, Situbolai said, "What do you want of me?"

"Give me men so that I may pursue Culchas and take back the fallen god."

Situbolai shook his head. No, princess," he said, pointing at the map. "One of his armies is camped outside of Nertobis, blocking our way. To the north, Culchas has taken Caiscata, blocking the northern road passing through Contrebia Leukade. His men have moved out of the Belli lands in the south, joining with their army,

53

so there is no way to know where they've taken the star."

Aia stood alone.

Situbolai motioned for his men to follow and with a glance at Caros, he departed.

Caros was angry. "Have you lost your mind, Aia? You shouldn't have antagonized Culchas."

"What are you doing here?" asked Aia.

Caros said, "We're here to renew an ancient covenant of peace between the Arevaci and the Titti people."

Now that the fallen god had been lost to the enemy, Aia became insistent. "Will you not fight, father? Our people possess steel. The enemy has only weapons made from iron. We can beat them on the field of battle. Haven't you ever dreamed of following in the footsteps of past heroes?"

Caros glanced at the Hellene before he spoke. "The Arevaci no longer seek glory or conquest."

"Goodness is a weakness," grumbled Aia.

Caros walked around the table and placed a hand on Aia's shoulder. "One aspect of love is that you must endure the hate and envy of others, without returning their poison in kind. If others injure you, you must resist the urge to harm them back. This is the mark of an enlightened leader."

Turning around, Aia shook off her father's hand. "When you don't punish those who make war upon you, they will only grow stronger."

Caros adopted a condescending tone. "Resistance is created by fighting. If you harm others after they offend you, you will feed the fires of conflict. If you react with patience and forgiveness, you will put out the fires that spread misery."

Aia made a motion and Urcaildu brought the chest over, placing it on the table. Aia opened it, revealing the head of Indortes, king of the Belli. "Culchas wants you to know that he's coming for us soon."

"So King Indortes escaped the firestorm," whispered Caros.

Forcing herself not to shout, Aia said, "The Sedetani only understand the language of blood and death. They respect only an adversary more ruthless than themselves. They despise qualities like gallantry, fair play, compassion and forgiveness."

Urcaildu chimed in, "This is true, your majesty. These qualities are for the Sedetani, a sign of an adversary's weakness and stupidity."

Hilerno grabbed a spear from one of his men and threw it at Urcaildu, impaling him in the chest. Urcaildu fell down and died.

Aia screamed and drew her sword, ready to attack the general.

Caros made a motion and two of his men restrained her. "You'd better leave, Hilerno."

The general glared at Aia and with a smirk on his face, turned to go.

When he reached the door, Caros called out, "General!"

Hilerno paused. "Yes, lord?"

"I may not need you to fight this war after all. Do not forget your place."

Hilerno bowed and departed.

Turning her wrath against her father, Aia shouted, "How can you permit him to murder one of our men, father?"

"Urcaildu spoke the forbidden words." Caros looked down at the map. "Besides, on the field of honor, Hilerno's standard is worth ten thousand men. There is no greater strategist among our people." He made a motion and the soldier released her arms.

Aia's voice turned cold. "I've seen entire villages destroyed by the Sedetani. At Burzao dead women and children lay naked in the sun. The words are true, even if you forbid them to be spoken."

Aristæus gave her a patronizing smile. "The uncultured soul will see what it wants." His face turned hard, as if a mask had been lifted away. "I will say this very simply, so that you both can comprehend my words with your limited minds. The world is changing. The enlightened peoples of Gaia are advancing and they cannot be stopped. Your world of passion will be consumed by the forces of the human spirit."

Aia put her sword away. "Enlightenment is a lie invented by foreigners to control us. The only way to beat our enemies is to be as ruthless as they are."

Caros shouted this time. "You're behaving like a savage, Aia."

The shocking intensity of her father's words had pierced her to the core. For an instant, she wondered if her father was right. She was a worthless beast without honor.

Aristæus softened his words. "If you succeed in defeating them with brutality, won't you become evil as well?" He shook his head. "Perhaps the Celtiberians are all animals that need to be caged."

Caros sobered up. "We are men, not animals."

"Only an enlightened society shall endure," spoke Aristæus. "Maybe it's time to make room for other tribes more worthy. There's little indication that your people will ever change." After uttering these words the Hellene left the room.

Aia and her father watched him go, but before she could say anything, she heard him mutter, "Where has my gentle daughter gone?"

Doubt entered Aia's mind. She was flawed and defective. Internal voices whispered words of condemnation. A shudder coursed through her body as she realized that she was on the road to becoming a cruel tyrant like Culchas. "Father —"

Caros glowered at her. "Get out!"

Aia met his gaze. "How will you defeat the Sedetani?"

"I shall outwit them."

"Don't outwit yourself."

* * *

Stars glittered in the darkness. To the south, the red glow had diminished. It was as if the departure of the fallen god had taken the fire out of the earth. Aia sat at a table outside a tavern, drinking. The tavern keeper was a master brewer, and his caelia beer went down cool on a hot summer's night. Laughter and merrymaking tumbled down from the citadel like water running off the side of the mountain.

After the gods were honored with sacrifice, the strongest warriors from both tribes swore their oaths. Then came the weapon dances—sharp and ceremonial.

Aia watched the fading light in the south, wondering where the fallen god had been taken.

Resigning herself to her fate, she tried not to think of her future life at Hilerno's side. She was surprised by the extent of his jealousy—and how far he'd go to keep others away. Her thoughts drifted back to a time before the wars, when happiness had seemed certain, and her life had belonged to another.

A tune rose from the tavern. Aia heard a man's voice, accompanied by a lyre. He was singing about the battles fought by the Lusones against the invaders. Entranced, she listened to the deeds of great heroes in a hopeless fight. Then she heard her own name called out in a song. Startled, she went to the door of the tavern to look inside.

The bard was a tall, broad-shouldered man outlined against the firelight. His features were sharp, his blue eyes catching glints from the hearth, softened only by a crooked, knowing smile. He sat cross-legged on a table beside a bowl of apples, the lyre resting easily on his knee. His words needled with song-smith's precision, weaving truth and insult into something the crowd could cheer. His song made a mockery of her exploits against the Sedetani at the battle of Burzao, though it left out many details:

She rode to Burzao without her host,
No banner flew, no battle boast.
A girl with blades and tangled hair,
Too proud to kneel, too wild to care.

Aia, Aia, fire so bright—
Burned like day, then fled the night!

Aia, Aia, fox on the hill,
She fights with tricks, not warrior skill.
Too quick to charm, too light to bind,
She left her father's name behind.

Aia, Aia, fire so bright—
Burned like day, then fled the night!
The men held fast, the women cried,
The Lusones fell, the brave ones died.
But Aia slipped through blood and bone—
The only soul to walk alone.

Aia, Aia, fire so bright—
Burned like day, then fled the night!

Aia, Aia, bold and sly,
The coward lives, the brave ones die.
She freed the slaves with cunning art,
But shame still clings to a liar's heart.

His voice grew softer, drawing the crowd close.

But hush the hall and still the flame—
It takes a fire to trick a flame.

The last line hung in the smoke and silence. Then a murmur rippled through the tavern as eyes turned toward the doorway.

A few men laughed. One repeated the line with a sneer.

The bard struck a louder chord and led them all in a rough, mocking refrain:

—Aia, Aia, fire so bright—
Burned like day, then fled the night!

Her face burned hotter than the hearth. She turned and walked back to her table, seating herself with her back to the tavern wall. The applause died slowly. Then came footsteps. She didn't bother to turn around.

The bard sat down at the table opposite her. Putting down his lyre next to another bowl of apples resting on the table, he waved over a barmaid. "Two mugs of caelia," he called.

The barmaid came over and placed the beer on the table with a sidelong glance at Aia, but when their eyes met, the barmaid looked away.

"A drink," he said, "for the one who's inspired my most popular song."

Now she knew how the Titti guards had heard of her.

Aia leaned back in her chair. "I'm surprised the song is finished. Wouldn't you like to know the rest of the story?"

"I take what I can, princess." He took a sip of beer. "I'm Abellio."

She picked up a mug and took a sip. "That's a strange name."

"My parents named me after the god of apple trees."

A wry smile touched her lips. "You're making that up."

Abellio returned her smile as he picked up an apple, cutting it open with a knife. "Why'd you run away at Burzao?"

"Because beating Culchas is more important than my honor."

Abellio held a slice of apple on his knife. "Have you beaten him yet?"

Frowning, Aia looked away, shaking her head. "I'm only a woman," she said,, bitterness edging her voice. "I must match my enemy's strength with ingenuity. That's the only way I can win against him."

"You sound like King Caros."

Aia chuckled. "Yes, he thinks he can outsmart Culchas." Her mood darkened. "My father is harder on his own people than on his enemies."

Abellio looked into her eyes with a penetrating gaze. For an instant, their spirits touched. "So, are you going to marry General Hilerno? That's what everybody is saying."

"Hilerno is not a great man."

Abellio's smile was intoxicating. "Yes, but are you going to marry him?"

Aia stood up, pushed his chair back and straddled Abellio. Taking the apple out of his hand, she took a bite. "No."

* * *

Aia awakened to the sound of an owl hooting. A cool breeze wafted through the open window, where sunshine drifted in, along with the sound of carts and horses moving through the town. Aia stretched. Pushing a light fur blanket off the bed, she sat up to look around the chamber. Abellio was nowhere to be seen. A spot of pink caught her eye and she noticed a wild rose lying on the pillow beside her, next to a note on a piece of parchment. In Celtiberian script, it read: Go win me a song.

Getting dressed, Aia went to look out over the town from the second story window, wondering where she could find Tekos.

The voice was a surprise. "Sleeping in today?"

Turning around, Aia saw a familiar woman sitting in a chair with her feet up on the table, a cup of wine in one hand. With her long brown hair and somber eyes, Aia recognized the silent girl who'd been next to Culchas when Aia had climbed out of the pit. Aia looked at the closed door, wondering how she'd entered.

In a matter-of-fact tone, the girl said, "Good morning, princess."

"How is it that you know who I am?"

"Your father told me." She put down the cup of wine and smiled. "I'm Saorla."

Saorla spoke with an Aquitanian accent, like Nescato. Aia crossed her arms, resisting an urge to draw a sword. "As a Sedetani spy, tell me why I shouldn't kill you."

"Oh, that would anger your father, wouldn't it?" Taking her feet off the table, she glanced at the bed. "I see you're quite good at running away from your troubles. Was he as good as he looks?"

Aia wondered how long Saorla had been following her. She didn't respond.

"How sweet," purred Saorla, "he left you a bouquet." Saorla

61

poured another cup of wine from a pitcher on the table. "Aren't you afraid of getting pregnant?"

Aia felt off balance. "Not at all," she murmured, "I've been taking silphium." Carthaginian merchants had brought the herbal contraceptive from across the sea. It was worth more than gold.

Sipping wine from the cup, Saorla smiled. "We all live in a world full of desire, don't we?"

"What were you doing in the company of Culchas?"

"Posing as a wealthy Aquitanian trader, I gather information and bring reports back to your father."

"Why are you here?"

"Your father stopped listening," grumbled Saorla. "Would you like to find the fallen star or shall I send in another man?"

Feeling the heat rise in her face, Aia narrowed her eyes. "Tell me."

"A Lusitanian priest by the name of Tyresius has taken charge of the fallen god. His dark tower stands in the town of Alaun, at the fork of the Iber and Salo rivers." Saorla put down the cup. "Of course, an army stands in your way."

"That won't be any trouble."

"I admire your confidence." Saorla stood up to leave.

"Why are you helping me?"

Saorla paused at the door. "Because Culchas is a savage," she said.

*　*　*

CHAPTER FOUR
The Magic Jar

Some say that the Keltoi have no gods because they have no temples. These primitive tribes worship in the wilderness, making sacrifices to nameless gods at night during the full moon, dancing and drinking until the dawn. It cannot be denied that the atheistic Keltoi are dangerous savages. In love with battle, they do not understand how deliberate violence is like a raging fire. If it isn't quickly put out, it will spread misery across the earth.

The Carthaginians, in their endless pursuit of wealth, are only interested in trade with the natives. So I took it upon myself to help these pitiable tribesmen, in the hope that one day they might live among the great nations of Gaia. I remain here, in Celtiberia, condemned to dwell among an inferior people until they understand what it is to be civilized. It may prove an impossible task. Barbarians will forever be ruled by their lusts and passions.

Princess Aia was a beautiful person once. Her descent into violence fills my heart with sadness.
— *The Chronicles of Aristæus*

The girl knelt under the shade of an oak tree, sobbing. Dark hair fell down over her face, covering her eyes. Barefoot, she had no belongings other than a white linen dress. Next to the tree, the Salo River flowed by, its surface as smooth as Persian silk. In the distance, smoke drifted up into the sky. Reflections of swirling vultures passed over the water.

Walking over green moss covering the exposed roots of the tree, Aia approached the girl. With a glance over her shoulder, she saw Tekos standing by the chariot some distance away, watering the horses while Nescato lay by the river under the shade of another oak tree lining the road down from Nertobis.

The girl ignored Aia, who sat down beside her. The girl's delicate face was covered in tears. Wind whispered through the branches, scattering shadows into patches of sunshine.

She raised a small white hand to brush her hair back. "They're all gone," she said.

"Who?" asked Aia.

The girl pointed at the smoke rising from behind a hill and then dropped her arm into her lap. Shaking her head slightly, she whispered, "Now who will come to see me?"

Taking the girl's hand into hers, Aia looked at the reflections in the river.

After some time, the girl said, "You need to go down before rising."

Aia released the girl's hand. "What do you mean?"

The girl gave no reply.

Shaking her head, Aia went back to the others. "You two ready?"

"Can't we stay here tonight?" asked Nescato.

Shaking her head, Aia considered Tekos. "That girl told me there's trouble up ahead."

"What girl?" asked Nescato.

There was no one sitting under the tree any longer.

Bewildered, Aia glanced up and down the road and over to the river but all was quiet. "There was someone here a moment ago—a girl next to that oak."

"You've been talking to a tree spirit," murmured Nescato. She looked up into the trees. "This is a sacred place."

Not bothering to reply, Tekos went back and brought up the chariot. Aia got in, wondering what she'd seen. They rode on for a time until they went by the hill, which had blocked their view. On the other side a broad plain swept down to the Iber River. The Salo River ran alongside the road that went down to meet it.

The scent of rotting flesh mingled with the odor of ash. Several hundred bodies were strewn about the ruins of a burning village. Stakes had been driven into the side of the road with heads impaled on them. Fire ignited in Aia's heart as they rode through the village. Taking out a javelin, she hoped they might encounter Sedetani soldiers, but the village was deserted.

* * *

The heat of the sun was cut down by the wind flying past the speeding chariot. Tekos was seated in the front, with Aia standing behind him. Nescato rode a horse a short distance behind. Vineyards grew along the side of the road, which ran through the Salo River Valley to the east of Nertobis. Up ahead, a roadblock manned by Sedetani soldiers barred the way. Aia put a hand on

65

Tekos' shoulder. "Let me handle this, will you?"

A pair of men stood in the way, armed with spears and tall oval shields painted in red and white. They wore helmets with cheek guards, and were protected by leather scale armor. A third man stood behind a barrier which blocked the road. As the chariot approached, one of the soldiers raised a hand. "Halt!"

After Tekos reluctantly brought the chariot to a stop, Aia smiled at the soldiers and spoke in perfect Iberian, "Greetings, warrior. Can you direct me to Orisos' command tent? I have good news for the general."

"Who are you?"

Raising an innocent eyebrow, Aia said, "Don't you recognize us?"

The guard threw a glance at the trio before shaking his head.

Stepping off the chariot, Aia approached the guard, lowering her voice. "We're scouts," she said. "We've just come back from a long patrol." She pulled out her sword, and showed it to the man. "See this? This is Carpetani steel." Aia handed the sword to the guard who examined the weapon with admiration. The other two guards came close to see it too. Aia pointed at Nescato, who glared down at the soldiers from atop her horse with an imperious look on her face. "See that girl? She's the daughter of the Carpetani king. She's to be Orisos' bride, and the king has agreed to arm us with steel weapons like this one as a dowry."

The leader examined Tekos with a critical eye. "That's not an Iberian chariot."

"Of course it isn't," said Aia. "Do you think we could pass through foreign lands undetected in one of our own chariots? We liberated this vehicle from the Belli. Ever since the star fell out of the sky, their entire army has been in disarray."

The guard gave Aia's sword back. "Fine with me," he said. "What's the password?"

Aia chuckled. "I said we were on a deep patrol."

"I understand," said the leader. "Tell me last week's password."

"I don't think you know how far Toletum is from here," said Aia. "It's beyond Ikesankom on the Tagos river."

As the man was about to speak, a javelin plunged into his chest.

Startled, Aia drew her other sword just as another soldier was struck by a javelin. The third man turned away to run but Tekos rode after him, impaling him in the back.

Aia scowled as the crossed into Sedetani territory. "I can't believe you did that," she grumbled. "I had them going. They would have believed me."

"The sun is going down," said Tekos. He got out of the chariot to retrieve his javelins.

"You just ruined a perfectly good lie." Aia frowned. "Are you always this quick to kill?"

"I don't see why you're so fond of sparing their lives," grumbled Tekos.

"Secrecy is my desire—to pass through their ranks without anyone noticing."

Nescato was impatient. "Can we go now?"

"You know—you could have chimed in," muttered Aia.

"I don't speak Iberian as well as you do," said Nescato.

With a loud sigh, Aia climbed into the chariot. She made a motion with her hand and gave a command, "Away then."

* * *

The dark tower stood atop a cliff at the confluence of the Iber and Salo rivers, next to the Sedetani town of Alaun. Wagons laden with supplies for the Sedetani army rumbled over the bridges. There were a great number of soldiers marching about in the sunshine. The lone chariot, followed by a rider, was conspicuous on the road leading up to the town.

"In Nertobis," said Nescato, "they say that Tyresius is a Necromancer, calling up spirits of the dead to do his bidding."

At last a bit of cover appeared up ahead. They approached a willow tree growing by the river. She noticed a ford where one might cross over to the south. A trail there joined another road which headed south to Salduie, the Sedetani capital, bypassing Alaun altogether.

"If Tyresius has come out of the west, he may have brought others with him." Aia glanced back at Nescato. "How good is your Lusitanian? I only know a few words."

Nescato tried to smile. "I speak it about as well as Iberian."

Shaking her head, Aia tapped Tekos on the shoulder. "Pull over there." She got out of the chariot. "How about you?" she asked him.

Tekos turned hawk like eyes towards the tower. "I'm not here to talk."

"That's what I thought," grumbled Aia. "If you cross here, you can bypass the town and meet me down river later tonight."

"Don't you want any help?" asked Nescato.

Aia shook her head.

Nescato was incredulous. "You're just going to walk right up to the dark tower?"

"Yes."

* * *

The sun was setting by the time she made her way down the final stretch of road. Aia came to a small market just outside the town gates. She acquired a pair of melons and a few precious yards of red Persian silk. Wrapping the melons up in the silk and tying it up with a bit of leather, she made her approach.

The tower stood apart from the walls of Alaun, as if the builders didn't want to associate with those living in the town. A flock of black crows circled high above, their calls echoing off the rocks at the base of a cliff that plunged down into the river. The distant rush of water came up to touch the tower, caressing the black stones and leaving a fine mist there. The wet ground made the trail leading up to the tower slippery.

Pausing at a well near the tower, Aia dipped her hand into a bucket in the hands of a serving girl and splashed water all over her own face. Before the girl could complain, Aia said with a smile, "Hot today, isn't it?"

Cursing, the girl tossed out the water and threw the bucket back into the well.

Walking as if she expected the silk bag might burst into flames at any moment, Aia carefully made her way over a small stone bridge and up to the entrance. A pair of Lusitanian soldiers stood by, wearing dark green tunics and helmets with black horse-hair plumes. They were armed with Celtic swords and spears and carried round shields made of wood, reinforced with iron.

Out of breath, Aia spoke in anxious Iberian, "This is the tower of Tyresius, isn't it?"

"It is."

Wiping the moisture off her brow, Aia handed the bag to one of the surprised guards and with a sigh of relief, said, "There you go."

As she walked away Aia heard the guard call out, "What's this?"

"Dragon eggs," she said, glancing over her shoulder at the distant conflagration in the sky. "They came out of the firestorm."

"What are we—"

Aia brought a finger up to her lips, shushing the man. "Quiet down. They're ready to hatch."

The guard whispered, "What do I do with them?"

"Culchas thought Tyresius could train them up, though I expect the dragons will burn down the tower." Aia turned to leave.

The guard held the bag out from his chest, as if it were a viper. "You take this inside."

"I wouldn't know where to go."

"It's easy," he said. "Just take it up to the top floor. Tyresius works there."

Wincing, Aia reluctantly took back the silk bag. "All right," she grumbled. "But if you hear me scream, stay away. No use in both of us getting killed."

When Aia came to a flight of stairs, she heard a lonely song drifting up from below. The solitary melody was a quiet tune wrapped in despair. It was beautiful and strangely compelling to listen to. Biting her lip, she looked up. Aia couldn't bring herself to ascend the stairs.

Drawn by the haunting melody, she descended instead.

There were six cells under the tower. They were all empty, save for one, which contained a lone girl who sat on the stone floor, singing to herself. Her wrists were bound in iron chains attached to the wall. No windows pierced the black stone walls. Illumination came from a set of bronze braziers spaced evenly down the corridor. As Aia approached, the girl looked up. Shadows slipped from her face when the light touched it.

She was a fresh looking young girl with long brown hair. She wore a dark blue dress made from fine linen and a pair of sandals. Her brown eyes were deep wells of sadness with a touch of fury. For some reason, Aia took an immediate liking to the girl. It was as if they'd been friends their entire lives. They smiled at one another.

Chains clinked as the girl brushed a strand of hair from her face. Her head tilted slightly as she regarded Aia. She said something in the Lusitanian language, but Aia didn't understand her words.

Speaking Iberian, Aia asked for the girl's name.

The girl shook her head, not comprehending.

Aia switched to Celtic, "What's your name?"

"Belexeia."

"Where are you from?"

"Val d'Aran."

The Aquitanian town was far to the northeast, beyond the great mountains. Aia glanced at the other cells, wondering why Tyresius held the girl prisoner. "Why—"

All of a sudden Belexeia stood up, reaching through the bars of her cage but the chains around her wrists held her back. One finger brushed across Aia's face, and it felt as cold as an icicle on a winter's night.

Surprised, Aia stepped back away from the cell. Involuntarily, she reached up to touch her face, holding a hand against the chill. The side of her face was numb for a moment, but the sensation quickly faded away.

"Help me!"

Aia shook her head. "No. I —"

"Please," implored the girl. "They're torturing me!"

Bumping into the bars of the cell behind her, Aia felt dizzy. She closed her eyes.

The darkness behind her lids was like the hush of a deep cave, and for a moment, she let herself rest in it. Her breath came slow and shallow. Her heart thudded like a distant drum, and she pressed her palm to her chest as if to steady it.

The gentle clinking of chains made Aia open her eyes again.

Belexeia was seated in the center of her cell once more, head bowed. "I'm sorry."

Aia lowered her voice, "I can't help you."

Belexeia remained silent. Sorrow pooled around her in the darkness.

With a shudder, Aia backed away.

To the side of the cell, a shadow stepped out into the firelight. Startled, Aia put her hand on her short sword, but stopped herself from drawing it.

Nescato stepped up to the cage. "I'll help you."

Irritated, Aia asked, "What are you doing here?"

Nescato pointed at the dark amulet around her neck. "Thanks to the Dark Queen, nobody can see me when I stay in the shadows."

"Where's Tekos?"

Nescato mumbled, "He said that he wanted to go have some fun."

Aia wasn't sure she wanted to know. "You're going to get us into trouble," she said, putting her hands on her hips. "Besides, we don't have the key to her cell."

Nescato chuckled. "Not to worry." She nodded towards the stairway. "I'll take her away from here. Go find your fallen star."

Aia hesitated. "This one's an enchantress."

"She's Aquitanian, like me," replied Nescato.

"She's not like you, Nescato. She's—" *Belexeia is dangerous.* Aia shook her head. "Never mind."

Picking up a wood tray that lay in front of Belexeia's cell, Aia covered it with the Persian silk and, taking out a knife, cut the pair of melons in two. Placing them onto the tray, she went up the stairs without another glance.

Pushing the door open with a soft touch, Aia stepped into the chamber at the top of the tower. A line of shelves filled with rolls of parchment swept in a curve halfway round the room, cut by a niche leading to a window. Another line of shelves covered the other side of the tower and these were filled with an assortment of jars and boxes. There were two other windows inside stone niches where one might look down at the town. The light from the distant firestorm mingled with the sunset, throwing a faint orange glow into the darkening room.

A large oak desk stood to one side, covered with a roll of parchment next to a beeswax candle, a piece of chalk, a ceremonial silver knife, a cone of burning frankincense, and a quill by an inkwell. A long spear made of iron engraved with silver symbols leaned against the wall. An intricate Persian rug covered the floor and several oil lamps hung from the ceiling. None of the lamps or candles had been lit, and shadows gathered in the chamber.

The corpse of a young man lay splayed out upon a granite slab to one side of the room, his arms and legs held fast within manacles of iron that were attached to rungs set into the corners of the stone. A shallow trough was carved into the circumference of the stone. There was a hole at the lower part of the stone and a bronze vessel stood underneath a spout carved into the image of a dog. A small table by the slab of stone held four earthenware jars with the heads of jackals. Strange colored signs and pictures were drawn upon the jars. Next to the jars, a bronze tray held a series of knives and strange looking implements. There was a tall pithos jar with a crystal sphere attached to the top. A luminescent orange liquid was suspended within the crystal sphere and a small cork ball floated on the surface of the fluid. Enshrouded in a white mist, a blue orb hovered above the stone slab, looking like a soap bubble that refused to drift away. A whimpering whisper issued from the orb, raining sorrow down upon the stone.

A thin man stood next to the granite slab, arms crossed, with one hand up to his chin. Intense dark eyes under shrewd black eyebrows gave him a fierce look. A lock of his untamed short black hair thrust into the air above his face. Clean-shaven, he looked about thirty. He wore a black tunic bound with a white belt and black boots. Aia thought him darkly handsome.

A young woman sat in front of a table by one of the windows, gazing out into the coming darkness. With long brown hair and dark scheming eyes, she wore a black dress and a wild assortment of jewelry. She had a thoughtful face and a knowing smile. Aia felt a vague chill of foreboding creep over her when she spied the woman. The table held a crystal sphere, a cone of burning myrrh incense, a silk bag and a shallow gold bowl filled with water.

The third occupant of the room was a strong warrior holding a long Celtic sword, made out of steel. Bare-chested, he wore a loin-cloth and sandals. He stood immobile, like a statue, but when Aia stepped into the room he turned a suspicious pair of eyes towards her.

Deep in conversation, neither the man nor woman took any notice of Aia.

In a dreamy, child-like voice, the young woman asked, "Why have you imprisoned the fallen god, Tyresius?"

The necromancer had an eloquent voice. "To prevent him from destroying the world in a divine firestorm."

The woman cooed out in a mocking tone, "He cares about the little sheep, he does."

"They are not sheep."

"You always call them that," she purred. "'They need to be guided,' you said. 'They need to be controlled, just like innocent little sheep do.' That's what you said."

Tyresius was exasperated. "What I meant was that simple mortals need to be protected."

In a dreamy voice, she replied, "He wants the sheep to be happy, he does."

He fell into his thoughts once again, answering her in a distracted tone. "Devotion to the gods is the only way to safeguard their happiness and their fate. Culchas shall conquer Celtiberia and I shall rule over all."

She stared out the window at the rising moon. The fiery conflagration in the distance was bathed in blue. "Will your spirit cage hold a god?"

Tyresius didn't answer. He glanced over at an amphora jar resting on the floor. A gust of wind brushed against it, throwing chalk dust into the air. A white circle had been drawn upon the floor surrounding the jar along with strange signs that reminded Aia of the Tartessian symbols she'd seen carved on the standing stones. The jar was painted with the image of a burning star falling out of the sky. Beholding the magic jar, Aia thought she heard a voice, but it was as soft as the breeze blowing through the chamber. Light faded from the room as the sun dipped behind the mountains.

At last, Tyresius spoke. "Culchas will come for it soon."

The woman laughed quietly. "Culchas will never possess the fallen god."

In the moonlight, Aia could see that Tyresius was alarmed. "What have you seen?"

Silhouetted in the window, the woman tilted her head. "I see a girl standing by the door."

Speaking an incantation in an ancient tongue, Tyresius waved his arm and all of the lamps and candles in the chamber ignited at once, throwing light into the room. Aia stood there, holding the tray with cold melons on top of it, trying not to shake.

Moving like a panther, the warrior standing to the side advanced on Aia, raising his sword to strike her.

Aia considered drawing her sword but chose to remain still.

A moment before the blow struck, Tyresius called out, "In the name of Neito, stop!"

The warrior halted, his sword only a few inches from Aia's head.

The young woman stood up and approached with a grin on her face. In a distracted tone, she gave an order to the warrior. "Withdraw ten paces, Avatar."

The warrior stepped back into the niche by the window.

Aia realized that her heart was pounding.

"What a pretty girl," cooed the woman. "So wild and savage looking, she is."

With a look of astonishment on his face, Tyresius gave Aia a slow look-over. "The words that I heard are true," he whispered. Taking a step forward, he recited words, as if from memory: "I shall send you a lovely, charming maiden with the face of a goddess." Tyresius glanced at the woman. "The fallen god has sent me a gift, Lilura."

A thunderbolt struck Aia—she knew that name. Aia turned away to cover up the angry look on her face and stepped up to the table where she placed the silk covered tray. "My name is Aia," she said. Recovering her senses quickly, she turned around and smiled at Tyresius. "I'm your new assistant."

"The fallen god sent you a present, Tyresius?" With a pouting face, Lilura stepped closer, speaking in a whiny, child-like tone, "No fair. I want a present." Lilura's eyes turned cold, sending a chill up Aia's spine. "Did you bring something for me too?"

76

Before Aia could respond, Tyresius interjected, "The fallen god sends gifts to whoever he pleases, Lilura."

A red glow ignited against the stone windowsill. Excited shouts could be heard in the town below. Tyresius moved over to the window and looked down into Alaun. Fire engulfed several buildings. On the hillside beyond the town, a flaming chariot drove by the walls. Fiery arrows flew out from the chariot like shooting stars.

Not taking her eyes off Aia, Lilura spoke. "It is a Seraph." She walked to the window, placing a hand on the wall. "The Burning One has come for the fallen god. The Seraph gains strength as the flames grow. Can you extinguish the fires?"

Tyresius looked down into the blazing town. "Not from here."

With a swift turn, Tyresius went out of the chamber, heading downstairs.

Lilura remained in the window, her white face illuminated by the fires.

Aia cast her gaze towards the magic jar. She thought she could hear music coming from it, no more than a whisper, inviting, drawing her in. The soft melody turned into a pair of words, barely discernible: "Release me!"

A stone thrown into a still pond, Lilura's voice was startling. "All of the blessings of humanity are sealed inside this magic jar, along with the fallen god."

Aia looked into Lilura's eyes and felt a strange thing there: Fear.

With a motion to the warrior, Lilura gave a command. "Dispose of her."

The Avatar of Neito advanced upon Aia, sword in hand.

Drawing her long Celtic sword from the sheath on her back, Aia retreated a step, blocking a sword thrust.

The Avatar threw a series of strikes, aimed at her chest and head.

Parrying all of the attacks, Aia moved in a circle towards the magic jar, knocking a chair out of the way. She tried a counter strike but her opponent leapt out of the way.

The Avatar struck like a serpent—sudden and lethal.

An opening appeared and Aia aimed a strike at his head.

Jumping backwards, the warrior brought his sword up to parry the attack and her steel sword broke in two.

Astonished that her sword, a weapon made out of Carpetani steel, could break, Aia tried to dodge his next strike, but she failed to do so in time.

Intense pain pierced her stomach. Aia felt her strength leave her and she dropped to her knees. A wave of dizziness sent her head reeling. It became hard to breathe.

With a grin on his face, the Avatar pulled his sword out of her stomach.

Aia remained there, kneeling, engulfed in pain, while darkness spilled into her eyes.

Lilura moved forward, her face filled with relief. She whispered, "Sometimes, an evil thing is cherished in the heart, but Tyresius shall never embrace you."

The Avatar of Neito kicked her in the head, and the world fell into darkness.

* * *

Aia knelt by an oak tree, planting rose bushes along the road-side that led up the hill to Arcailicos. Wildflowers grew over the fields on the other side of the river like scattered pieces of a rainbow. Thunderclouds drifted overhead, sending great purple shadows across the land.

Galloping hoof beats approached.

Aia stood up just as a rider came down the road. Startled, the gray horse came to a sudden stop, throwing the rider onto the ground. She smiled down at Karbelos. He didn't bother hiding his annoyance. Though she laughed out loud, her heart was beating as fast as the horse had been going.

Karbelos got up, brushing clumps of mud off of his brown leather tunic. "What is it with you and horses?" He was angry, but a smile crept into his face just the same.

"Where were you going in such a rush?"

He looked away into the distance.

Aia walked over to retrieve his horse, taking up the bridle. Stroking the horse on the nose, she waited for his reply.

Karbelos went to the side of the road, dropping down next to the rose bush. He touched one of the thorns. "I've never seen these kinds of flowers before."

"The king's advisor, Aristæus brought them out of Persia. I thought they'd look nice growing by the road." She smiled at the long line of rosebushes she'd spent all day planting. "He said they like the sunshine."

Karbelos grew silent at the mention of the king.

Aia sat down beside him. "What's happened?"

He picked up a clump of grass and threw it into the road. "My father has made a treaty with your king."

She leaned back onto her hands. "Is that such a bad thing?"

Karbelos nodded. "My father has asked me to marry the princess of the Areveci, as a token of friendship with your people."

There was a flash of light. A crack of thunder came down from the sky.

Aia brushed a strand of hair out of her eyes. "You don't want to marry the princess?"

Karbelos shook his head. "My heart belongs to another."

Rain came down. The oak tree gave little shelter, and the cold water ran in rivulets down their faces. Their eyes met, a patch of sunshine hidden in the dripping rain. He got up and went over to lean against the tree trunk. "They call her the 'Princess of Flowers,'" he grumbled. "She's probably fat and ugly."

Aia grinned.

Turning around, Karbelos brushed the drenched hair out of his face. "What?"

* * *

Opening her eyes to a world of pain, Aia groaned. Hard wood pressed against her face. She lay face down in a pool of blood. Fire dripped out of her stomach and she writhed in agony. All of her strength had gone. It was as if she was a flower withering in a dry vase. Wind blew through the tower, sending out a cool touch against her skin. Light danced across the floor, cast down from the ceiling lamps. Other than the murmur of the wind, the room was silent.

A golden glow spread out across the room. Curiosity undefeated, she managed to turn her head to see what had caused the illumination. The magic jar was surrounded by gold light, as if it had been dipped in sunlight. A lonely murmur came from the jar, calling out.

Summoning all her remaining strength, Aia crawled forwards, towards the magic jar. Pain tore at her stomach with each movement. Trailing a pool of blood and fire, she fought against the blackness spilling into her eyes. By the time she reached it, she was utterly exhausted. Reaching out, her finger brushed against the magic jar.

There was a low hum. Warmth spread throughout her body. The pain melted away like frost in the sunshine. Life returned. Aia rolled onto her side and brought herself up into a sitting position, arms around her knees. All remnants of pain seeped away. Inhaling cool air, she stood up, an athlete ready for another race.

Aia wondered at the magic jar.

A whisper: "Freedom!"

Was it the wind?

The door to the chamber burst open. Lilura came inside, followed by a pair of Lusitanian soldiers and the Avatar of the war god Neito. The woman came to a sudden halt, mouth agape. The warrior drew his sword and advanced with the slow precision of an executioner.

Without a thought, Aia ran over to the windowsill, glancing down into the Iber River.

Lilura found her voice, shouting this time, "Kill her!"

Aia dove out of the window into the river, plunging down into the chilly water. Rising up to the surface, she spied the moon going down behind the dark tower. She could still see the golden glow in the window. Divine fury contained within a magic jar—with a touch of warmth.

Aia narrowed her eyes in determination. "All of the blessings of humanity," she grumbled. "In *their* hands!"

The golden light faded from the tower window.

Aia let the water carry her away into the night.

*   *   *

CHAPTER FIVE
The Sword of Auruningica

Cold wind blew across Aia's wet skin. She sat shivering on a carpet of grass near a raging fire, not caring if the light might draw the attention of Lusitanian or Sedetani soldiers. Tekos draped a blanket made from rabbit pelts around her shoulders. It brought a touch of warmth to her face. The moon had gone down, but a red glow still lingered over the town, whispering of the fires that had scarred it.

Candlelight illuminated a pair of bewitching eyes in the darkness. Belexeia sat cross-legged under an ancient oak tree, singing softly over a white candle. Though it was summer, the melody reminded Aia of a cold winter's night.

Aia closed her eyes.

As she floated in the river, a rumbling sound came up from behind. Turning over onto her stomach, Aia tried to swim to the river's shore, but the rapids drew her in. Uttering a prayer to the river goddess Iberia, she turned onto her back again, letting the water carry her away down river, hoping the swift current wouldn't dash her across sharp rocks or hold her underwater. The roar of the river erupted around her and she was swept under the surface, choking and gasping for air. Something sharp cut her legs and arms and she felt herself plunging down into the cold depths. After a time, strong hands drew her limp form out of the river. Gasping for breath, Aia didn't care if she'd been caught by the Sedetani. But gentle hands placed her on the ground. She looked up into Tekos' warm eyes.

Nescato's voice brought her back to the present.

"Great thinking," grumbled Nescato. "You find the fallen god—who you say has been sealed inside a magic amphora jar—and what do you do?"

"Stop it, Nescato," said Tekos.

Undeterred, she continued, "You jump out the window!"

Shivering, Aia responded through chattering teeth, "There wasn't time."

"You said you were right next to it."

Aia wondered how many people would suffer because of her mistake. Drawing the furs closer around her shoulders, Aia stood up, trembling in the glow of the raging fire, trying to forget the look in the Avatar's eyes.

"Was it too large to carry?"

Shaking her head, Aia looked down into the fire. "It was no taller than my knee."

"So why didn't you take it with you? All you had to do was grab it on your way out."

"If it bothers you that much," grumbled Aia, "why don't you just sneak back into the dark tower yourself and steal it."

"Maybe I'll just do that."

84

"Try if you dare," mumbled Aia.

Tekos emerged from the shadows. Firelight flickered in his eyes as he gazed off into the darkness. He tilted his head, as if he was listening to something. "The night does not belong to you, Nescato. You cannot return to the tower."

Wondering at his words, Aia was reminded of Faiatura. The Dark Queen's amulet could be dangerous if Nescato used it too often. She shook her head. It would be impossible anyway, what with the entire town of Alaun on alert.

Aia turned away from the warmth and walked out of the firelight, where she cast her gaze into the black forest. Lucent vapors drifted up to the edge of the flickering light, lingering there. A chill swept down Aia's back and the hair on the back of her neck stood up. Several luminous shapes drifted past, whispering and chattering. A macabre face appeared out of the mist, its pale eyes searching. Despite the fact that they were all out in the open, the shade didn't seem to notice them. After a moment's hesitation, it swirled away back into the misty night.

Aia realized that she'd been holding her breath. Glancing at the others, she whispered, "How is it that they can't see us?"

"Candle magic protects us," whispered Nescato, who'd come up besides Aia. All irritation had gone out of her voice. "Belexeia is an enchantress."

Listening to Belexeia's song, Aia shivered. "She's a Brixta—a witch."

"That's what I said."

Ghostly shadows crept past their sanctuary. Pale eyes sunken into bleached white skulls, searched the forest. They carried spears and swords that came from another time. Their shields were decorated with the images of forgotten gods and writing that came out

85

of Atlantis. There were hundreds of them. A tall white figure stepped into view, leering into their camp. Aia could see the fire dancing in its eyes. The phantom stood there, unmoving.

Instinctively, Aia reached for her long Celtic sword at her back, but it wasn't there. The Avatar of Neito had broken her weapon back in the tower. Taking a step back, she drew her short sword from the scabbard hanging from her belt.

Nescato put a hand on Aia's arm, gently lowering it. "They're already dead."

Not accustomed to feeling helpless, Aia put her sword away, trembling against the cold.

The phantom's eyes darted to and fro, searching. Sensing their presence, it sniffed the air like a hound. But it came no further into the firelight. Aia fought an urge to run away into the night.

Replacing Aia's sword with an earthenware cup, Nescato brought up a jug, pouring cool liquid into it. "Water from the shrine of the river goddess," she said. "Drink. It will calm you."

Aia glanced down at the cup in her hand. "I've had enough water from the Iber River." She looked up into the eyes of the phantom. It glared back at her, unseeing. "The necromancer has summoned evil spirits to search for us."

"Tyresius sent them to look for *you*, not us," said Nescato.

The phantom turned towards Nescato at the mention of the necromancer's name.

All of a sudden a gale issued out of the west. The candlelight flickered and went out. Belexeia coughed and stopped singing. The glow of the fire flickered off the wispy spirit, who turned to look directly at Aia. It let out a hiss and moved closer, reaching out with one hand.

A scream escaped Aia's lips and she fell backwards. Without

thinking, she flung the water from the cup into the phantom's face. There came a shuddering cry that sent a chill down her spine. The phantom faded away, dissolving into blackness.

Aia lay on the grass, listening to her racing heart.

"I'm sorry," said Belexeia. "I'm engaged in a fierce battle with Tyresius and Lilura." Belexeia took a deep breath and shook her head, as if to clear it. "Tyresius commands an innumerable force of eternal spirits. Once our swift pursuers discern an advantage, they shall tread us down."

Aia stood up, staring into the night. The trees caught the wind, sending a murmur through the forest. "Lilura commands magic powers?"

Belexeia nodded. "Yes, Lilura is a Druidess, a Seer. She's trying to locate us." The candlelight returned. Belexeia started singing again. The feeling of protection returned like a warm blanket.

"So, what do we do now?" asked Nescato.

Not answering, Aia returned to warm her hands at the fire.

"I suppose we could all go home," prompted Nescato.

Belexeia stopped singing for a heartbeat. The candlelight flickered. "No!"

"What will Culchas do with the Magic Jar?" asked Tekos.

"He will conquer all of Celtiberia," said Aia.

Placing a bowl before her, Belexeia made a motion towards Nescato and while the girl filled the vessel with water, Belexeia placed another candle on the ground, igniting it. "I won't permit him use it." She began to sing a new melody, though nothing seemed to happen.

Nescato went over to a natural spring which came out of an outcropping of rocks in the side of a hill and refilled the water jug. "Why should I care about Celtiberia?"

"The Sedetani will conquer the Aquitanians too," said Aia. "I think Culchas wants to rule over all of the Celtic tribes."

Firelight danced off the water in Belexeia's bowl. Images appeared in the water. Aia saw Lilura sitting at a table in the dark tower, gazing into a ball of crystal. Smoke from burning incense curled around her face. Night mists had formed into the wispy shape of a phantom illuminated by the moonlight coming from the window. Tyresius stepped into view. He threw an irritated glance at Lilura and then he spoke to the phantom. "Find the one named Aia and bring her to me. Kill the others." The phantom grinned and floated out into the night.

With a sharp intake of breath, Lilura had a look of surprise on her face. She cast her gaze about their chamber, searching. "The witch is spying on us." She picked up a wand made from ash and waved it in the air. A moment later, she leered directly at Aia and a smile crept across her face. She waved the wand again. Aia felt Lilura's touch, like a feather against soft skin. Lilura sought an opening into Aia's mind.

Whispers emanated from the magic jar, pushing Lilura's mind away. There was a scream, and Aia felt the seer's presence fade away entirely. Warmth came out of the magic jar, reaching out, searching, until the god touched Aia's mind.

There was a blinding flash. The world spun round. She felt herself falling into emptiness.

* * *

After a time, Aia rose onto her knees, blinking. A strong gale threw her hair into her face. Brushing it aside, Aia saw that she was on a mountaintop. The sun was high up in the sky. A woman wearing a golden crown emerged from a circle of massive stones in a valley below. She strode forth, accompanied by a retinue of warriors.

88

Aia stood up and looked down from on high. Ten thousand warriors were drawn up in ranks on the mountain slopes next to their horses. The woman with the crown drew a sword from a jeweled scabbard and raised it high over her head. The army cheered. With a song on her lips, she stepped into a white chariot and she rode forth, followed by the army. On horses swifter than any Aia had ever seen before, they rode on into the green valleys below. Their songs faded away on the wind.

Blinking away the vision, Aia awoke. The sun had emerged from the underworld and was now climbing into the sky. Nescato knelt beside her with a curious expression on her face. "What did you see?"

"A queen on the mountain." Aia looked at The Three Mothers.

"There's a shrine up there, dedicated to Epona," said Nescato. "It's a vision from the goddess."

"She had a magnificent sword in her hand." Rising from the ground, Aia noticed that the others had all fallen asleep. Belexeia looked exhausted. Aia turned again towards the mountains. "I must acquire it."

Nescato looked up at the mountains. "Why?"

A smile curled into Aia's lips. "Use the weapon of a goddess to defeat a god."

* * *

Unable to travel at night for fear of the Dark Queen, they rode under the hot sun. Belexeia said that her candle magic would protect them from discovery but the night phantoms pursued them in the darkness, making it difficult to rest. Aia didn't want to rely on the witch's magic but she didn't see another way to escape from Sedetani territory. Giving in to whatever fate the gods chose to bestow upon her, Aia led them up into the hills to the south of Burzao where they encountered ruined towns, burned crops and always, the corpses of those slain in the war. Most of the fair women had been taken away, so the bodies were of children or the elderly. Occasionally they encountered dead warriors near a burned-out village. Although they were rising higher every day, Aia felt as if she was descending into a nightmare.

One evening while they camped at the base of the mountain, they sat listening to Belexeia singing. Nescato looked into Aia's eyes. "Why are you on a quest for glory? What's so important about greatness?"

"My people do not respect me."

Nescato laughed out loud. "So?"

Narrowing her eyes at the girl, Aia remarked, "We are not alike, you and I."

"You are a thief," stated Nescato, "but I am more clever than you."

"I'm no thief," protested Aia. "I'm..." but her words faded away into silence.

"You don't even know what greatness is." Nescato got up and walked away from the firelight into the darkness.

Tekos came over and sat down next to Aia. "We cannot take the chariot higher up the mountain from here," he said. "The forest is too dense. I suggest we swing around to the south and approach the mountain from there."

"Very well," she said. The fire seemed to glow brighter around Tekos. She wondered if she would be able to find the shrine from her vision. "My father would say that civilization leads to greatness," murmured Aia, "but those ideas come from his Hellenic adviser." She looked at Tekos as fire danced in his eyes. "What say you?"

"Why is it so important to you?"

Aia cast her eyes into the glowing embers. "I wonder if I'm worthy to wield the sword of a goddess," she whispered.

Tilting his head, Tekos listened to the darkness.

"What is it?" asked Aia.

The horses standing next to the chariot neighed in surprise. The snapping of underbrush came from the trees surrounding their camp. Dozens of soldiers emerged from the forest. Tekos stood up and raised his golden spear. Belexeia stopped singing and Nescato drew her knife. Just as Tekos was about to throw his spear, Aia shouted, "Wait! They are my people."

Reluctantly lowering his spear, Tekos glanced at Aia, but she wasn't looking at him.

A company of Arevaci soldiers came into the light, led by Hilerno himself. "In my experience, greatness is an illusion."

"What are you doing here?" asked Aia.

With a smug grin on his face, Hilerno walked into the camp, surveying her companions. His eyes rested on Tekos. Aia saw a reflection of the fires burning there. "Your interference has become a distraction for the king, Aia. Your father is concerned that you will bring more dishonor to the Arevaci. So I've come to take you back to Titum."

"I've been banished." Aia knew it was only an excuse. She was banished from the lands belonging to the Arevaci, not the Titti.

"You will apologize to your father and all will be well," he said. "Then you shall return to Arcailicos to await my return."

The thought of her returning home was repugnant to Aia. She had no intention of accepting a life of dishonor and mediocrity at Hilerno's side. "How did you find me?"

Walking over to inspect the chariot, Hilerno surveyed the rest of the camp with a critical eye. "We've been following your progress from the magic map inside King Situbolai's palace. You just missed the departure of the Sedetani army. Before your arrival, they marched north from Alaun Most likely, they're headed towards Kalicoricos and presumably, Vareia."

Aia wondered how she could warn the Berones people. She had no doubt that Culchas, aided by the fallen god, would defeat King Ultinos. How many people would die?

Hilerno looked inside the chariot and disappointment spread into his eyes.

"You've come for the fallen god!" accused Aia.

Hilerno chuckled and made a motion. Arevaci soldiers emerged, leading a line of Sedetani warriors, who came into the camp with smiles on their faces. A particularly burly Iberian with an ugly beard stepped up by the fire to warm his hands next to Aia. Tekos stepped in front of her protectively. "I have been ordered to escort these warriors back to their lands," intoned Hilerno. "You were merely a stop along the way."

Narrowing her eyes, Aia felt a firestorm rising from her heart. How could her father release these prisoners back to their enemy Culchas? Madness had clouded the king's mind. She glared at the general. "These hills belong to the Lusones, not the Sedetani."

"King Olónico has been conquered," said Hilerno. "You said so yourself that Turiazu has fallen to the Sedetani army."

At the general's signal, soldiers moved in.

Tekos stilled. A fire stirred beneath his skin. His jaw clenched. Fingers curled. A silent ember glowed, ready to flare.

Aia placed a hand on her companion's arm—cool, steady. He turned to her. Their eyes met, and she saw the fire behind his gaze. A shadow of a smile slipped across her face.

He exhaled, the tension in his shoulders easing.

With a single, sharp nod, he let the soldiers lead him away.

A faint scent of smoke lingered.

Hilerno glanced around the camp. "You never found your fallen star, did you?"

Aia crossed her arms, not willing to indulge his curiosity. She glared at the Sedetani warriors, lowering her voice. "How can you release them?"

"Come now, princess. You don't want to interrupt the dance between Culchas and your father. The party has only just begun." Hilerno and his men settled into their camp. "You'd best get some rest tonight. I intend to return you to your father tomorrow in Titum. We will celebrate the festival of Litha together there. If you want more say with our people, marry me."

* * *

Aia lay on her side some distance away from the crackling fire, unable to sleep. A wolf howled in the distance. What prey did they hunt tonight? Rather than feeling safe and secure, surrounded by warriors from her home, Aia knew she was trapped. How she wished to run with the wolves, free. Tomorrow she would be taken away to live in a gilded cage by Hilerno's side.

A cool breeze touched her skin, carrying with it the unmistakable aroma of apples. Without warning, a strong hand came up over her mouth from behind. Before she could react, a gentle shushing sound was followed by a familiar voice. "Do not be startled, princess."

Surprise melted into elation. Resisting an urge to roll over and slap him—or to give him a kiss, she whispered, "Hello, Abellio."

Carefully, they slipped away from the camp into the night. Aia wondered what had happened to the sentries, but there was no time to inquire. She remained silent while he led her a great distance away into the forest.

Sitting down in a clearing under a wild apple tree, Abellio spoke first. "Tekos and your other companions will make a break for it soon." He laughed. "They'll lead Hilerno and his men away on a merry chase through the wilderness."

Relieved, Aia sat down. She looked up at the crescent moon rising over the mountain, igniting the silver fires of his enchantments. The wolves howled, closer this time. Gazing into his eyes where hunger roamed free, her grin was wild and mischievous. "You think I'm beautiful?"

"Like dawn running naked through a field of sunflowers," he muttered, his eyes burning like those of a wolf. He put his arm around her, and leaned in. As their lips touched, Aia gave way to a hunger of her own.

A moment of bliss only, and then she drew away.

"What's wrong?"

"Wait," she said, trying to catch her breath. At the same time, she wanted no more than to be devoured in ecstasy. She gazed spellbound. His dark hair caught the moonlight and dazzled her. Silver fires burned in his eyes. He reached out.

"No!" She stood up, moved a pace away and leaned against the apple tree.

"We're perfectly safe here," he said.

Running a hand through her hair, Aia shook her head. "It's not that." A sliver of the moon rose over the mountain, framing him against the stars. "Did you plan this?"

Abellio laughed. "Of course. I followed Hilerno and his men out of Titum when I learned he was looking for you."

"You said, 'Go win me a song.'"

He leaned against the tree trunk, obscuring the moon. "You

94

have."

"No," she protested. "My quest isn't over."

His face was close to hers, intimate. "And what quest is that?"

"To defeat Culchas."

Abellio pulled back. She resisted an urge to reach out. He stepped away. "With every person who has ever lived, there is a summer which shall never come. You are a warrior, Aia. Glory in the summers that remain."

Abellio was a magnificent lover, and knew how to utterly exhaust her passions. She shook her head. "I must keep up my strength for the trials to come."

He laughed. "What trials?"

Aia looked up at the mountain. A cloud drifted across the moon, plunging the world into darkness. "This isn't a game, Abellio."

"All life is a game." He moved close again, and leaned in for a kiss. "Tonight, we shall live. Tomorrow, let darkness fall wherever it may."

Aia pushed him away. "No."

* * *

The chill dawn awoke Aia, who rolled over and looked up at the blue sky. Abellio had gone away, leaving her alone on the side of the mountain. Rising up, she was surrounded by mists climbing into the sky. It was as if the world was about to catch fire.

The ascent took all day. Out of breath, Aia reached the summit and cast her gaze around the mountaintop. To the west, she could see the distant fortress of Numantia, where King Magavárico ruled the Pelendones tribes. It lay beside the Dubro river, which flowed south and then west, past her home, Arcailicos. To the north lay Contrebia Leukade, another fortress of the Pelendones that guarded the northern pass into the lands of the Celtiberians. Turning back towards where she had come from, to the east, lay the dead towns and villages of the Lusones. Smoke ascended into the skies from the destruction there. The southern skies were covered in dark ash emanating from where the star had fallen. Unseen, Titti stood in a hidden vale, brooding under scarlet skies.

Aia could not find any sign of the place she'd seen in her vision. Defeated, she sat down on the mountaintop. A chill wind blew, scattering the summer heat. "What am I doing here?" she wondered aloud.

Thirsty, she went down in search of a spring. After some time, she heard the sigh of flowing water and discovered a spring that opened up onto the side of a cliff which fell into a forested pool. Climbing down, she quenched her thirst and rested upon a rock, wondering what to do. Closing her eyes, Aia remembered the words of the druid Piresso: *As long as the mists of doubt envelop you, be still. Wait until the sunlight burns away the fog. Then go forward with courage.*

The unmistakable sound of movement through the forest rose over the rush of water. Opening her eyes, Aia stood up, listening. The neighing of horses came through the trees. Aia walked through a maze of green until the pine trees opened up onto the side of a wide grassy plain descending down the mountainside towards Numantia. Close to the edge of the forest where the stream emerged, Aia saw a dark maiden dressed in black. She had a crown of geraniums in her black hair. Surrounded by a dozen horses, she held a wicker basket full of apples. She was feeding one to a mare when Aia emerged from the trees. The maiden ignored Aia as she approached but when Aia was a few paces away from a foal, the maiden spoke. "Why have you come?"

"I seek a beautiful sword that I encountered in a dream," said Aia, "born by a warrior queen at the head of an army on the side of this mountain."

The maiden laughed and the sound of it was sweeter than the music of silver fountains, and poisonous with cruel derision. "You speak of Auruningica. The queen and her people lived among these hills long ago."

"Do you know where Auruningica's tomb is?"

The maiden gave Aia a forbidding look. "Queen Auruningica rests in a glittering cavern under the mountain." She turned away. "But I will not show you."

"Why not?"

The maiden's laughter was biting like the chill mountain stream at their feet. "You could no more wield the queen's sword than you could ride this mare."

A smile crept into Aia's face. "I have tamed horses more wild than this in my life."

The maiden slapped the mare's rump and the horse galloped away. "Go on then!"

Aia ran down the hill after the horse, followed by the maiden's laughter.

It took quite some time for Aia to catch up to the horse. She waited until the horse looked in her direction and then withdrew a few paces. Aia called out, inviting the horse to approach, but the mare moved away. "You don't want to come to me," said Aia, "but since you don't want to do that, you need to do this…" Aia waved her arms and shouted, "Go away!"

The horse galloped off.

Aia approached again, got the horse to look at her and invited the mare to come over. The horse ignored her. So Aia began the

97

process of chasing her off, then inviting the horse to approach. Eventually, the mare decided that she'd rather come over than repeat the game.

Mounting the horse with a sense of satisfaction, Aia looked up the mountainside where the maiden stood, watching. Suddenly the horse bucked and threw Aia to the ground. The maiden's laughter streamed down the mountainside next to the splashing brook.

Standing up, Aia looked at the setting sun. "This may take some time," she grumbled.

Aia continued to try all night but was unable to accomplish her task. As the embers of dawn rose over the forest, she sat down, defeated. Rubbing a sore shoulder, Aia wondered how many times she'd been thrown to the ground. The horse whinnied from just over a grassy rise, taunting her.

"You win," she moaned. "Perhaps I'm not worthy." Grabbing a clump of dewy grass, she tossed it into the morning breeze which blew hair into her face. Aia prayed aloud, "Epona, I wish only to restore my honor, and to protect my people!"

There was a touch at the side of her head. The mare had returned. Smiling, Aia stood up and ran a hand down the horse's neck. A moment later, Aia mounted the horse. She rode up the hillside in search of the maiden, but the girl was nowhere to be found.

Aia searched all day until, hidden inside a grove of trees, she discovered a massive circle of standing stones. It looked as if they'd been cast down by the gods to lie scattered, naked in the hot sun. Aia approached one massive stone and ran her fingers along the warm surface. She walked around the stone with her hand against it until she came to a shadow cast by an overhanging tree limb. The shadow was cold, having drained all of the sunshine away.

Suddenly, her foot met empty air, and Aia tumbled down into

a cavern through a hidden hole at the base of the standing stone. Striking the hard earth, she grunted in annoyance. Rising from the ground, she looked about a glittering cavern covered with quartz crystals. The beam of light falling through the hole scattered into a million rainbows. At the back of the cave there was a shrine, carved into the likeness of the warrior queen Auruningica. An earthenware urn filled with ash stood at the base of the shrine.

Upon a massive crystal at the foot of the shrine lay a sword.

Emerging from the glittering cave, Aia inhaled a fresh breeze with renewed vigor. She climbed back to the top of the mountain as the sun was going down. Taking up the sword, she began to practice. As she twirled in a circle, she felt as if she was riding a whirlwind. The fading sunlight scattered off steel, flashing her eyes. Her mind wandered down the mountain slope like a rock falling onto the plains. She imagined that she heard the distant sound of horns and marching feet. Far away, a cloud of dust rose into the air, approaching Contrebia Leukade, the town guarding the mountain pass. Clouds of sacred birds came down like a fog of death.

The invasion of Celtiberia had begun.

*　　*　　*

CHAPTER SIX
Night Phantoms

Riding down the mountain at night, Aia was surrounded by stars. It felt as if she was riding out of the River of Heaven, descending into a world covered with night mists. Emerging from a grassy plain covered with dew, she found the road leading from Caiscata towards Contrebia Leukade. Pausing a moment on the road to listen, she wondered how long it would take the Sedetani army to catch up to her. Glancing back up to the mountain, she was amazed. She had traveled twice as fast as she should have in the descent. Running a hand along the horse's mane Aia asked herself if it was the magnificent horse or the magic sword which gave her such speed. With a shrug, she turned left onto the road and brought the horse into a canter.

After a short while, a huge shape formed out of the mist ahead. It was a green hill, surmounted by the fortress of Contrebia Leukade. Two concentric walls ten feet thick and a line of towers protected an inner fortress made out of stone. The road split off onto another path that swept up the hill in a serpentine manner all the way to the top. Inhaling the fresh air of dawn, she made her way to the summit, where she passed through the unguarded gateway into the city. Just as she entered, the rays of the rising sun surrounded her.

Aia felt the heat of the sunlight, which seemed to have followed her into the fortress. Sleepy residents moved about the town like shadows in the mist. Though many stopped to gape, no one approached her. Ignoring them, Aia focused her attention on a great stone that stood in front of the gateway to the inner fortress. Covered in ancient writings, it reminded her of the stone she had passed on her way down to the inferno.

A soldier who held a tall red shield and a spear, challenged her.

"I am here to see King Magavárico," she said.

The man laughed. "Go away from here!"

"I bring cruel tidings."

"The way is shut."

"No it isn't," she muttered. Glancing at the open gate, Aia kicked her horse into a gallop.

"Hey!"

Riding through the gateway up to the fortress, Aia leapt off her horse and walked towards the stairs that led to the entrance. A shout erupted from the fortress and a contingent of soldiers appeared. Not quick enough to reach the stairs before the warriors, Aia drew the sword of Auruningica from the leather scabbard on her back. Dawn light glittered off steel as she took up a fighting stance.

As if struck by a thunderbolt, the warriors halted.

A heavy voice, tinged with annoyance, came down from a balcony overlooking the courtyard. "Who is this?"

The guard, out of breath, said, "No one, lord!"

Before he could continue, she shouted, "I am Aia, daughter of Caros of the Arevaci. I have come down from the mountain." Gazing up at the man, she raised her eyebrows. "Who are you?"

"I am Lord Elguismio, chancellor to the king," he said, rubbing a hand on his chin. "The daughter of King Caros?"

"Did you know that the army of Culchas approaches from the east?"

Elguismio's mood darkened. "Come inside."

* * *

Their footsteps echoed through the passages. The fortress was empty. Lord Elguismio led Aia through the stronghold and out a back exit. A trail led up to a beautiful garden protected by high walls near the top of the hill where an enormous boulder stood overlooking the fortress below. Walking over stepping stones separated by creeping thyme, the laughing sounds of children grew louder as they approached.

King Magavárico reclined on a couch, watching a dozen children play in the garden. As he came into view, Aia couldn't help but smile to herself. The music from a fountain floated into the air where songbirds whirled around in an intricate dance. They came to a stop next to the king, who caught a ball thrown by a little boy. As he threw it back out onto the field, he turned a curious gaze in Aia's direction. Lord Elguismio introduced Aia.

"The Princess of Flowers." King Magavárico waved Elguismio away. "What do you think of my garden?"

"It's quite beautiful." Taking a seat next to the king, Aia bit her lip. She didn't want to bring bad news.

His next words surprised her. "You should not have come here," he said. "A Sedetani army advances out of Caiscaita."

"You know of it?"

"Scouts have brought news out of the east."

Aia looked at the garden full of youngsters. "Will you send the children away to your fortress at Numantia?"

"Whatever for?" he asked. "This stronghold is too mighty for the king of the Sedetani."

"Culchas has acquired great power," she warned. "Tyresius, a Lusitanian Necromancer in his service, has imprisoned a fallen god inside a magic amphora jar."

Magavárico laughed. "It is not possible to imprison a god."

A sudden gust of wind swept through the garden, causing a pair of wind chimes hanging from the branches of an elm tree to dance. When the gale had dissipated, Aia noticed that all of the birds had stopped singing.

The silence was broken by Magavárico, who stood up. "In any event, I cannot ask my people to run away in dishonor."

Aia rose from the bench. "Then I shall stand with your people."

Magavárico smiled. "I welcome your assistance."

* * *

Aia stood on the roof of the tallest tower in the fortress, gazing out over the battlements at the coming gloom. "They say that men of the Pelendones have keen eyes that can see a sparrow in a tree on the other side of a field. Nabarosin, what can you see on the road from Caiscata?"

"I see shapes moving in the darkness along the road. What they are I cannot tell. Night has not yet darkened the valley, but a shadow falls where the sun still shines. Something greater than an army approaches," he said. "Come, let us go down from this tower."

Nabarosin was a man from the royal guard who was assigned to give Aia a tour of the defenses. He wore a white tunic, a round breastplate and a Celtic helmet surmounted by a black horse hair plume. His equipment was like most of the other Celtiberian warriors: A spear, a curved falcata sword and a tall oval shield painted with blue geometric symbols. Many of the warriors also wore amulets around their necks, made from fragments of clear crystal. Though most of the men had a complacent attitude, there was a tenseness in the air, like shadows growing in the fading light. Aia wondered if they were unafraid of death of if they were simply overconfident. But something lurked at the edge of her memories as they descended the tower and went out into the street.

Nabarosin interrupted her musings, "I must leave you for a time. The enemy is expected to arrive here just after sunset. Where will you stand?"

"I shall defend the main gate, alongside you."

Nabarosin smiled and went away.

Aia retrieved the horse she'd tamed on the mountain and led her down to the town gate. "No need for you to die here. Return to the maiden on the mountain." She slapped the rump of the mare and the horse galloped away into the hills. Turning about, she went back into town.

A familiar voice appeared from the side of the road. "You're so good at meeting men, princess, but what have you done with your chariot driver?"

Aia saw Saorla, her father's spy. The woman sat at a table in front of a drinking house, sipping wine. Aia crossed her arms. "Why do you care?"

"Oh," she said, running a hand along the rim of her drinking cup, "he's the prettiest one of your boyfriends, that's all."

"He's not my—" She shook her head. "What are you doing here?"

"Same as you: waiting for the Sedetani to arrive." Saorla drained the cup. She refilled it from an amphora jar.

Aia sat down. "Where are you from, anyway?"

Saorla poured another cup of wine, offering it up. "Iaka."

"That was an Aquitanian town. It was destroyed by the Sedetani, wasn't it?"

Saorla ignored her curiosity. "After you failed to acquire what you were looking for, Culchas decided to invade Celtiberia, before you might try again." She grinned. "Got his attention, you did."

It was Aia's turn to drain her cup. She looked away at a group of soldiers sitting on the rim of a wall. They were eating bread and cheese. Carefree laughter fell down at her feet.

How would Culchas use the magic jar? She closed her eyes, remembering how it had taken her wounds away. It had saved her life. Lilura's laughter came to mind, along with the Seer's distant words: *Culchas will never possess the fallen god.*

"I'm glad he's not here," Saorla continued. "I wouldn't want Tekos to suffer from your mistakes."

The sun was going down, throwing shadows into the streets. "If you like Tekos, why don't you talk to him?"

It was Saorla's turn to look away. "He takes no notice of me," she whispered.

"Then make him notice you."

A raven haired woman lurked in a distant doorway. Dressed seductively, she attracted the attention of a passing warrior. A familiar laugh drifted up the street. The woman took off a pendant, put it around his neck and they went inside.

Aia stood up.

"What is it?"

"Lilura is here."

"Who?"

"A woman I saw talking to Tyresius."

"I'll take my leave now."

As Saorla slipped away, Aia felt her spine tingle as a dark realization touched her mind. How many warriors had she seen wearing Lilura's amulets?

Aia took off at a run.

* * *

Aia reached up to the amulet hanging around Nabarosin's neck, ripping it off. It felt like a ball of ice and she dropped it into the street. A cold whisper emanated from the crystal. Nabarosin had a quizzical look on his face. Aia looked into his eyes, seeing the fog begin to clear away. "Call up your men."

In the distance, beyond the walls of the fortress there came a rhythmical sound like rain falling on the rocks. At first it was only a whisper. After some time it had drowned out the sounds of the city. Finally, it grew into a storm of marching feet, accompanied by chanting and singing. An army advanced like an approaching thunderstorm.

Aia and Nabarosin raced about the fortress, pulling off the enchanted necklaces wherever they found them. All the while the sound of the marching army grew louder and louder until it was like a tide breaking across the walls of the fortress.

The Sedetani army had arrived.

Aia went up to the top of one of the towers connected to the main gate. In the distance, she could see the Sedetani army drawn up in orderly ranks beyond the range of their archers. Red light from the setting sun glinted off their helmets and spears like thousands of flames ready to ignite an inferno. At the head of the army stood three horses. General Orisos rode next to a pale-faced man wearing purple and white robes. A sultry woman sat astride a black horse next to them. Lilura had left the city to join the Sedetani army.

"Where is Culchas?" muttered Aia.

"Does it really matter?" said Nabarosin. "I have the Sedetani army at my front. Let King Magavarico deal with the rest." He called over a runner. "Go inform the king that Culchas is not here and to keep watch." The man took off at a run for the upper fortress. Nabarosin smiled at Aia. "Now we see how strong our defenses are."

A horn sounded and a lone rider broke off from the Sedetani army to approach. He came up to the front gate, halting within shouting distance. "Lord Culchas of the Sedetani claims this town, along with all the lands north of The Three Mothers. Will you submit?"

Nabarosin shouted, "No army has ever broken this gate or breached these walls. Go back to your master. Take your warriors back east, or they shall not see another sunrise."

The rider rode away.

"Why do we bother talking?" he muttered. "Let's get on with it."

Orisos made a grand gesture and his army advanced.

A leader next to Nabarosin shouted, "Archers, stand ready!" The line of men on the walls drew arrows from quivers.

"Draw!"

The Sedetani army marched closer. There came a distant shout and they raised their shields, forming a roof over their heads and a wall at their front. Aia had seen the Sedetani moving in such formations before. It was a Carthaginian tactic. Now she knew who the rider was next to Orisos. It was the strange man from Carthage. Orisos had called him Baalhaan.

"Shoot!"

The sky was filled with arrows from the defenders. Most of

108

them struck shields, but a few found targets. A horn blast came from the Sedetani army and they came rushing forward. Aia glanced at the setting sun, which was obscured by a dark cloud rising out of the ranks of the enemy. "Look out!"

Arrows landed everywhere like raindrops. Aia and Nabarosin took cover behind the battlements of the tower just in time, but several of his men were struck and fell. A moment later, ladders came up, followed by a rising tide of men. Nabarosin ran over to the nearest ladder and pushed it away from the wall. Screams rose up from below, but they were interrupted by a thumping noise from behind.

Aia turned and saw two men climbing onto the tower roof. Drawing both of her swords, she faced them down. One burly Iberian stopped to stare at her. The other one drew a mace and came at her. Aia parried his attack with her short sword and swung her other sword down upon the man's helmet, splitting it open.

Another pair of men climbed out onto the roof. Aia kicked the first man in the chest, pushing him off the tower and she slashed at the other one. He parried her strike, but his sword broke. She stabbed him and turned around to face the Iberian, who was rushing at her back. Stepping to the side to avoid a thrust, she sliced out with her short sword. He collapsed, clutching his side. Recognition filled her with surprise. It was the Iberian prisoner who had stood beside her warming his hands while Hilerno taunted her about her love of greatness.

A loud rolling noise came from below. Aia ran over to the tower battlement and looked down. The gate was open. A pair of defenders stood there, in a daze. Crystal amulets glinted from their necks. Cursing, Aia ran down the stairs and out into the street where the gates stood open, naked to the enemy. A company of enemy warriors broke formation and sprinted towards the gate.

Aia raised the sword of Auruningica. The last glimmer of the fading sun shone off the sword, throwing light into the gap. The flash stopped the men as if they'd struck a wall. Whether it was surprise or fear, she couldn't tell. Orisos rode forward into the gap, halting in front of her.

"Come on," she taunted. "What are you waiting for?"

Orisos gazed at her in wonder and surprise. "It is you. Aia of the Arevaci." He waved at his men. "Take her."

As if a spell had been lifted from the company of men, they came rushing forward.

The reality of her approaching doom struck home. "Too many," she said. Turning around, she retreated into town. A pair of warriors threw spears at her. Dodging them, she rushed back and killed them both. A dozen men tried surrounding her and she killed them as they came at her, striking out with both swords. Soon, a pile of bodies lay around her. The road through the gateway was covered in crimson.

"Culchas should have killed you," said Orisos. "I will, now."

Galloping forward, he thrust a spear.

Stepping to the side, Aia grabbed the spear, pulling Orisos off his horse.

He got up and drew a sword.

A horn sounded from over her shoulder. Friendly warriors rushed up, surrounding her. Orisos ran back outside. Soldiers led by Nabarosin shut the gate.

"Not today," she said.

The sounds of battle faded to silence. The defenders moved about with water and bandages for the injured. Aia stopped a man carrying a bucket. The water cooled the fires in her heart. She wondered what her father would say if he knew that one of the prisoners which he had released had nearly killed her.

Darkness came with the setting sun. Nabarosin came over to her side. "I do not understand why the enemy has halted their assault."

"Let's take a look." They ascended a tower and gazed out onto the Sedetani army which had retreated beyond a hill. As the last red shadow faded to black, there came a low wail from the field, a cry of loneliness mingled with hate. Aia felt a chill run down her spine. In place of the army stood a woman. A pale glimmer shone from her face, even as the darkness spread around her. The woman raised her arms and Aia saw luminous spirits of the dead rise up from the corpses littering the battlefield. She took a step back.

Aia felt Nabarosin's hand on her shoulder and realized that she was trembling.

"It is Ataecina, Goddess of the Night."

"What?"

"She has come to devour the city," said Nabarosin. "You need to warn the king."

The word came unbidden, an automatic response dictated by honor. "No."

Nabarosin shoved her. "Go!"

Night phantoms advanced upon the fortress like an oncoming windstorm of despair. Aia stumbled down the stairs in a daze. When her feet touched the earth she glanced over her shoulder just as luminous vapors descended from the top of the wall. Turning round, she fell onto her back. The vapors formed into the shapes of warriors. The defenders tried fighting, but their weapons met empty air. One by one, they met grim fates, screaming in terror.

Aia found herself on her feet, running away from the darkness which pursued her. The cries from the town ignited her panic. Before long, she was pounding on the door of the fortress.

No one opened it.

Sensing a presence at her back, Aia turned around. She was face to face with Ataecina herself. The goddess reached out, whispering, "Give me Nescato!"

On pure instinct, Aia drew the sword of Auruningica and slashed. As soon as it struck, there came an earsplitting shriek. It felt as if she had plunged her sword into an icy lake. Aia's arm went numb and her heart froze. She dropped the sword, blinking away fear. Ataecina was no longer there. Aia leaned against the door to the main fortress listening to her rapid heartbeat. There came a cold gale out of the west and the cries of terror from the town drifted away, until silence covered the town. The phantom host had faded into oblivion.

Unexpectedly the door opened and Aia fell onto her back. A warrior reached out to help her to her feet but she didn't take his hand. Aia picked up her sword and stood. Pins and needles washed over her arm.

The warrior was terse, "Come."

He led her to the tallest tower of the fortress which overlooked the garden. Most of the city's women and children took refuge there, since it was the safest place in the city. Magavárico stood in the tower, looking away from the battle, up at the top of the hill. Aia wondered what he was staring at. "The fight is in the other direction, Your Grace."

"You are wrong, Princess."

Squinting her eyes, Aia saw a large force of men gathered at the foot of the hill, beyond the tall gate that shielded the garden. A bonfire lit a clearing where an amphora jar rested next to a thin man.

Tyresius stood, arms crossed, resting his chin on one hand. Firelight reflected off the well muscled torso of another man as he approached the magic jar. It was Culchas, King of the Sedetani. He reached out to touch the magic jar. Despite the distance, she thought she could hear whispers drifting over the wind. Aia closed her eyes, wondering what gift the fallen god would bestow upon her enemy.

"What is he doing?" asked the king.

Aia opened her eyes and saw Culchas moving up to the top of the hill where the huge boulder rested. "No, no, no," she muttered. Turning to the king, she warned, "You need to get away from here."

King Magavárico laughed.

There came a fierce grunt from the hilltop. Culchas pushed against the boulder. Magavárico's laugh caught in his throat. Culchas was moving the stone. There came a thunderous roar as the massive boulder came crashing down the hill, followed by a roaring crash as the boulder smashed through the garden wall. There was a moment of awed silence. Triumphant cries burst out from the Sedetani army. Rushing down the hilltop, they climbed through the breach, cutting through defenders like wolves among a flock of sheep.

King Magavárico drew his sword. He glanced at Aia. "You!" he shouted, "Get out of the city while you still can." His grim smile was followed by softer words, "Give your father my thanks, for sending his daughter to visit me."

The king turned his back and led his bodyguard down into the garden.

* * *

The rushing wind whipped Aia's unbound hair around her back. She felt her heart beating in time with her horse's racing hoof-beats—until a second set pounded rapidly from behind. Laughing, she glanced over her shoulder at Karbelos, who rode in her wake.

113

Turning her head forward again, she spurred her horse on, but his horse was faster. Like a bird, he swept past, grabbing the gold medallion in her hand as he did so.

She could hear him laughing and he turned his horse to race down another garden path into the valley below Arcailicos. Setting her sights on his horse, she raced after him, throwing up clods of dirt in her wake. As they came to a bend in the road, his horse slowed down, obviously tiring out. Aia smiled to herself, knowing that her own horse had greater endurance than his. Spurring her horse into a faster gallop, she reached out and snatched his medallion out of his hand.

Aia slowed her horse to a canter and rode down a slope to the Dubro River, where she halted. Getting off her white horse, she smiled as Karbelos rode up and dismounted.

Aia smiled. "Now, who's the greatest one of all?"

He looked irritated. "Come on, Aia. My father gave me that medallion."

"Really?" she taunted, "Why would King Olonico give this to such a poor rider?"

His expression made her giggle.

"Give it to me."

"Not until you say it."

He tried to grab the necklace, but she was faster. "Nope."

He stood still for a moment. "You are."

"I'm what?"

Karbelos tackled her to the grass, but she wouldn't let go of it. He tried to open her fist, and she could feel his strength winning out. So she kissed him. His hand went limp as he kissed her back. Aia rolled them both over until she was sitting on top. She raised the medallion into the air. "Say it!"

114

"You're the greatest one of all, Aia."

Getting up, she dropped the medallion onto his chest. Sitting up, he put it around his neck as she sat down beside him. "You give up too easily," she complained.

"I don't believe in fighting," he said with a grin on his face.

Returning his smile, she lay back against the grass. "Me neither."

The sun was climbing high into the sky, bathing them in warmth, but he seemed to sense her uneasiness. "What?"

"I wonder sometimes how we'll build a better world," she mused. "Most kingdoms have evil rulers like the Sedetani."

"Your father isn't evil," he said, "and neither is mine."

Aia rolled onto her stomach. "That's what I love about you. You're a good man."

"But something is bothering you."

She grabbed a clump of grass and tossed it into the wind. "What about the rumors of the Sedetani army gathering in Salduie?"

"King Culchas has never marched this far north." Karbelos lay down, gazing into the sky. "His wealth comes from trading with the Carthaginians."

"He wants more than trade and wealth." Aia looked into his kind eyes. "Will you fight, if he comes?

"No."

"Our people won't respect you. They see your kindness as a weakness."

"Kindness is not a weakness, Aia."

"Yes it is."

Karbelos sat up and looked down into the river. "We all have a beast inside of us, ready to break free to spread hatred and death. I have no wish to become a monster."

Aia awoke to the sound of a little boy screaming. The cellar was hidden beneath one of the smaller towers of the fortress. She lay hidden behind a stack of crates, cradling her weapons and listening to the horrible shrieks that came in through the barred cellar windows. The boy's scream was cut short, followed by harsh laughter. Aia closed her eyes. "I can't take it anymore."

Morning sunlight filtered into the room from the outside, mocking her. Aia couldn't shake the feeling that she was being punished by the gods for her cowardice. Made to listen to the miseries brought down upon the unlucky survivors. "I have failed my friends and I have failed my family," she said. "I'm not worthy of anything."

Time to leave. Rising, she crept to the ladder that led to the ground floor of the fortress. Sheathing her weapons, she climbed out of her hiding place. Music greeted her as she crept through the fortress in search of an unguarded exit. There were none. Thinking of getting a better look outside so that she could devise an escape plan, she climbed a staircase to a small tower.

The clinking of coins greeted her as she approached a high chamber. Drawing her sword she stepped inside cautiously. Baalhaan the Carthaginian sat at a table, grinning. Stacks of gold and silver coins filled the tables around him, along with a treasure trove of wealth: Gold and silver goblets, bolts of fine linen and silk from the Far East, Persian rugs, fine jewelry and more. It was as if all of the wealth of the Pelendones tribes had been gathered into the room. Aia wondered how it could have been left unguarded.

Baalhaan's smooth voice interrupted her thoughts. "That's a beautiful sword you have there."

Aia glanced at the other exits.

"Would you sell it to me?" he asked.

116

"What?"

He was rubbing his thumb and forefinger against a small black stone in his hand. "Why do you fight?"

She moved to the window, looking down into the fortress. "To defend the honor of my people."

"Ah yes. The noblest spirit is always drawn to a love of glory." Baalhaan chuckled. "You barbarians are all alike."

Another scream rose from the courtyard where she could make out a line of children who'd been tied to posts and filled with arrows. Baalhaan spoke, "They're calling him the Lord of Massacres."

"Who is that?"

"General Orisos."

"Not Culchas?"

"No, he has gone from here."

She raised her eyebrows. "He took his army west to Numantia?"

"No. The Seer Lilura, has had another vision. So he's returned east."

"Perhaps he knows that General Hilerno of my tribe has gone north with an army to aid the Berones tribes," she lied.

"Hilerno's skill as a general is legendary. Didn't he once destroy two armies arrayed against him?"

"Yes. He stopped the Vaccaei tribes at Rauda. While they were engaged in battle he took half of his army north to Sekobirikes, and he defeated an army sent from the Turmodigi."

"I remember you," he said, "You climbed out of the pit of fire where the god had fallen. You're one of the Arevaci."

"Yes. I remember you too." He'd wanted to sell her into slavery.

Baalhaan smiled. "Now I have touched the Magic Jar and I am rich because of it."

Aia gestured with her sword. "Come with me."

"You want to use me as a hostage?" Baalhaan grinned, as if it was all a game. "How quaint. Do you think Culchas will care what you do with me?"

Aia hesitated for a moment, started towards the exit and then stopped. Baalhaan had gone back to counting his wealth. "Why aren't you trying to stop me?"

"Oh no. That would be against the rules."

* * *

The road west to Numantia was deserted. At the crest of a hill she stopped and looked back east. Contrebia Leukade had fallen to the invaders. The road was open. Now, Culchas would come against her people. Gray clouds drifted overhead, spreading darkness over the valley. A chill wind came out of the west, cooling her back and throwing hair into her eyes. Gradually, the wind was replaced by sounds of an approaching chariot.

Drawing her sword, she turned around. Sunlight glittered off the helmet of the chariot driver, who held a golden spear in one hand. Fire burned in his eyes. A dark haired girl stood inside the chariot, holding the railing, as if she was afraid to fall out onto the road. The chariot halted, throwing dry grass and dust into the air. The girl coughed.

"That's a nice sword," said the driver. "Where did you get it?"

Aia lowered the sword in relief. "Tekos!"

Nescato got out of the chariot. Admiration filled her eyes. "So, you were successful?"

Sheathing the sword, Aia walked over and got into the chariot. "What's the hurry?" asked Nescato.

With a nod, Aia motioned towards Contrebia Leukade. Whispers of a rhythmical sound, like falling rain, grew louder. Her lie to Baalhaan about Hilerno leading an army up north hadn't had any effect. "They come."

* * *

They rode through green hills and deserted villages full of stone buildings towards Numantia, their backs warmed by the summer sun. The rumbling sounds out of the east had fallen to a whisper and it was drowned out by the singing birds. After an hour, they came to a line of cypress trees lining the road next to a field of sunflowers. Tekos steered the chariot to the side of the road, halted and got out. He walked around to the front, attending to the horses.

"Why are we stopping here?" asked Aia.

"They need rest," he said, but Aia noticed his eyes wandering into the trees.

Aia followed his gaze and saw a pair of black horses tied up to a pair of cypress trees. Nescato went over to a beautiful mare, who whinnied a greeting. "Hello Iluna," she said.

Both of her companions were acting strangely, as if they were afraid to tell her something. Aia too, was afraid to mention what had happened the night of the battle. Ataecina, Goddess of the Night, had called out for her friend. Aia walked over to the second dark horse and ran a hand over his neck. "Nescato…"

The name caught in her throat.

Belexeia was sitting with her back to a tree, silent. Her eyes stared into the field of sunflowers, not seeing their beauty. She was trembling.

Forgetting Nescato for the moment, Aia went over and knelt down. "Belexeia?"

Belexeia dropped her eyes, not answering.

Nescato spoke, "We were looking for you, but she would go no further. She asked us to leave her here." Nescato's gaze swept out to the east where smoke ascended from the ruins of Contrebia

119

Leukade. As if in answer, the rhythmic drumming of marching feet drifted over the wind like distant waves washing against a shoreline.

Belexeia looked east, hearing the approaching army. Aia recognized the look in her eyes. It was a desire to ride west, to get away from the storm, to ride and ride and ride until the sea stopped you and then to go out into the water to swim away as far as you could go. "We have to get out of here," whispered Belexeia.

Aia stood up, hands on hips. "So stop them."

For the first time, Belexeia looked at Aia. "What?"

"Is there no spell?"

Belexeia shook her head.

Aia was insistent. "You stopped Tyresius and a host of evil spirits from finding us for days, and you say there is no spell you can use to stop a mere army of men?"

Belexeia was trembling. "No."

Aia stood and returned to Tekos, who had finished watering the horses. The fire in his eyes had gone, fading as the sun went down. She wanted to run too. How could they ever stop Culchas and the fallen god? She looked at the sky where sacred birds wheeled and danced in a sea of blue. "Let's get away from here," she said.

"Wait." Belexeia stepped into the road. Her eyes hardened in defiance.

Aia raised her eyebrows.

"You came from the conquered town," said Belexeia, "What have you seen?"

"They murder children in the streets." Aia crossed her arms. "I told Baalhaan the Carthaginian, that Hilerno was gathering an Arevaci army and were heading north."

"Baalhaan is an advisor to King Culchas," murmured Belexeia.

"He didn't seem to care about our army," grumbled Aia.

120

"They're not afraid of us."

A smile crept onto Belexeia's face. "They will be."

Gathering up herbs, incense, and black candles from her saddlebags, Belexeia knelt down into the road. She drew signs with a piece of chalk, lit the incense and candles. The sounds of marching feet in the distance blew through the trees.

Belexeia began to sing.

*   *   *

CHAPTER SEVEN

Steel

The Celtiberians are a strange people. They are in love with violence. Loud-mouthed and impulsive, they are ready to go to war at the slightest offense. These barbarians demonstrate that man is indeed an animal, whose nature must be enlightened by living in a civilized society, a polis. A lover of wisdom, Pythagoras, who lived on the island of Samos, once said that there is a good principle which created order, light, and man, and an evil principle which created chaos, darkness and women. Princess Aia has become a hindrance to her people and to her father, who has nonetheless demonstrated an interest in a society of education and democracy. King Caros even allowed me to create the Ekklesia, where citizens might speak their mind, but he insists on giving citizenship to inferior females. Indeed, their women have as much say as their men. Truly, they are a lost people.

— The Chronicles of Aristæus

Tekos led the chariot down into the lands of Celtiberia. A flood of fleeing people washed down from the fall of Contrebia Leukade. Yet their progress was unhindered. They came to the first fortified town surrounded by a high stone wall in the afternoon of the first day. As they drove up, a pair of sentries in red tunics, white cloaks, and bronze Celtic helmets with cheek guards stood in their way. One took up his spear and readied to throw it while the other challenged them. "Halt! Where do you hail from?"

"We come from Contrebia Leukade," answered Aia. "The city fell yesterday to the Sedetani. King Magavárico is dead."

The sentry looked dubious. "It is two days ride from there. How can you know of this?"

Aia glanced at Tekos and the team of horses, who did not look tired at all. "I saw it. I stood there with the defenders."

As if he no longer feared them, the sentry lowered his spear. "Why have you run away?"

"The king sent me to Numantia."

The other sentry smiled, incredulous. "You spoke to King Magavárico?"

Nescato, who rode next to Belexeia on a horse behind the chariot, said, "Enough of this! May we pass through town or not?"

"Certainly." Grinning, the sentries waved them through.

Aia was irritated but said nothing.

"You could have made up a more believable story," complained Tekos, as he led them into town and out the far gate.

"For once, I tell the truth and they don't believe me," she grumbled. "Perhaps I'm losing my touch." She glanced over her shoulder. "I didn't realize we'd traveled so far so quickly."

When the town had dwindled in the distance behind, they made their way through an oak forest. Golden sunlight filled the skies bathing the world in warmth. Singing birds drowned out the noise of the chariot as they rode on. After a time they emerged from the forest and went into a field of green grass that overlooked the Dubro River. The road split in two directions that followed the river north and south.

"Which way?" asked Tekos.

Aia glanced down at the wide river, whose surface was as smooth as Persian silk. She knew how deceptive it could be though, with strong currents underneath. "North."

They came to an unguarded bridge made out of stone, no doubt a design that came from Aristæus. After crossing over, they soon reached the great city of Numantia, which stood on a high bluff. Warm sunlight covered their approach to the city. As they drew near, they found an army encamped outside, down below the fortress. Aia put a hand on Tekos's shoulder and he halted the chariot.

A large force had assembled on a field to practice marching in formation to the tune of drums and music. Tribal colors identified different war bands, and their shields were covered with Celtic designs. It was a beautiful sight.

As Nescato spoke, her voice was full of wonder. "Wow!"

Aia smiled at the host of the Arevaci. "My father is here."

* * *

A sacred grove of trees grew in the middle of the city. No buildings had been erected there. It was a sacred place in the heart of Numantia. To Aia's dismay, an arena of stone had been constructed next to the sacred grove, so that people could look down into a fighting pit from where the ancient trees grew. Lord Elguismio stood next to King Caros.

Aia got out of the chariot and walked up to her father. While

125

Tekos remained, Nescato and Belexeia rode into the city. None of the soldiers protecting the king made a move to stop her. "What's going on?" she demanded.

Caros had a distracted look on his face, but he replied all the same. "Oh, hello Aia."

Lord Elguismio looked at Aia in wonder, surprised to see her again.

"Culchas has invaded Celtiberia. King Magavárico and the city have fallen to the Sedetani," said Aia, turning to Elguismio. "You are now the king of the Pelendones."

Elguismio did not respond.

"How can this be?" Caros too, was stunned. "Aia! You've run away from battle again. There was no need. Contrebia Leukade is unconquerable."

What did her father think of her? She was a coward without honor. Aia shook her head, to toss the idea out of her mind. She went on the offensive. "The fallen god aids Culchas in his war of conquest. King Magavárico sent me here with the news of the city's demise."

They did not respond. Was it fear?

Aia gestured towards the arena. "So, what is this?"

Elguismio emerged from his thoughts. "Soon, warriors will compete here for honor and glory. We have erected this arena as a dedication to Neito."

"The Sedetani war god?"

Caros nodded. "Yes."

Her father had finally lost his mind. "Sacred places are found, not created," said Aia. "You know that."

"That is why we built this arena next to the sacred grove," explained Elguismio.

"Yesterday morning, I watched as they murdered children in the name of their war god."

"Impossible," protested Elguismio. "How could you have traveled here so quickly?"

Aia drew her sword and it glittered in the sunlight.

Her father was astonished. "Where did you get this blade?"

"I found it inside a glittering cave beneath The Three Mothers," she said. "It is stronger than Carpetani steel. A maiden on the mountain told me where to find it."

Caros frowned. "A maiden?"

"There is a sacred grove dedicated to Epona there," said Hilerno. "The goddess of horses."

They all turned to see that the general had arrived, along with the Hellene Aristæus.

Aia put her sword away and smiled at Hilerno. "I'm glad to see that you brought the Arevaci war bands."

"It was a provocative action," said Caros, "but Hilerno thought it prudent, in light of the activity in the mountain pass."

Aia put her hands on her hips. "Activity?"

Caros crossed his arms. "We are not at war, Aia."

"How can you say that, while you stand next to friends who have bled and lost in battle?"

"I shall leave you to discuss this." Elguismio bowed. "I have to prepare my people for the arrival of our foes."

As they watched him go, Aia noticed the conflict in her father's eyes. She smiled. "Imagine the glory of defeating Culchas and the fallen god which aids him. With my sword, I can give you this victory."

"We can negotiate a treaty," said Culchas. "End this the peaceful way."

127

Aia shook her head. "No. We need to kill Culchas. We need to kill the Sedetani and destroy anything connected with their evil gods. They are a foul, cruel people."

"The Sedetani have always been foul," said Hilerno.

Caros was silent for a moment before he spoke. His words were cautious, as if he didn't really want to know the answer to his question. "How many people have they killed, Aia? How many children?"

Aia closed her eyes. "They stack the bodies in piles along the sides of the roads."

Caros shook his head. "So much violence fills my heart with sadness."

"In battle, I met one of the prisoners that you released," said Aia. "He nearly killed me."

Like storm clouds gathering in the gloom, darkness fell upon the king of the Arevaci. "Very well," said Caros. "Hilerno, summon our war leaders."

"You can't be serious. Not after all of the progress you've made." Aristæus had been standing by, forgotten.

"It appears that Culchas wants war, Aristæus. We shall defend ourselves."

"A man's character will define his destiny," said Aristæus.

Culchas took a deep breath before he spoke. "I have accepted the challenges presented to me. Soon, I shall feel the exhilaration of battle. Glory is mine for the taking."

Aristæus frowned. "You listen too much to this hot-headed girl."

"My daughter," said Caros.

"A mere woman." The Hellene shook his head. "I thought you had potential. Apparently I was wrong."

128

Caros glared at his adviser. "How can you say that? We've embraced your ideas, your philosophy. I have learned the virtues of restraint. I even banished my daughter in the hope that one day she would embrace your ideals, along with her honor."

"Yet she stands here," grumbled the Hellene. "Is this a real banishment?"

"She has been exiled from Arcailicos and the lands of the Arevaci," said Caros. "This fortress city belongs to the king of the Pelendones. Moreover, if she does well in the coming battle, I shall consider her honor price paid. She will no longer suffer the dishonor of exile."

"While my people and the Carthaginians are building great empires, your people will still be murdering each other over your silly quarrels," said Aristæus. "The Persian god kings out of the east can summon immense forces. That is the power of civilization."

Aia was too stunned to speak as she watched her father argue with the Hellene. Had he regretted exiling her? As she beheld him, she realized that his mind was made up. Caros and Aristæus glared at one another. Silence crept into the clearing. A cold wind blew out of the west and threw Aia's hair into her face.

By the time the general spoke, the Hellene society in Celtiberia had already crumbled away. "Yes, civilization is a great tool," interjected Hilerno. "It's also an instrument of power."

"We are more enlightened than you," said Aristæus. "The quest for power is not the reason to build a civilized society."

Hilerno chuckled. "Yes it is. The more you understand things, the more you want. The more you want, the more you take. Knowledge leads to aggression and a desire for power over others. Civilization is a wonderful tool to keep the people in line."

Aristæus shook his head. "I see that I have wasted my time here among you."

They watched in silence as he departed.

King Caros spoke first. "I am not certain that I agree with your assessment of a civilized society, general."

Hilerno bowed. "I am but a simple barbarian, Sire."

"You are a soldier," said Caros. "One day, Civilization will do away with your kind, too." He glanced at Aia. "Let us ride out to fight the Sedetani. I have no desire to stand behind walls to await my fate."

"What of the arena, this shrine which we have built?" asked Hilerno.

"Destroy it." Caros smiled. "With Elguismio's permissio, of course."

King Caros finally noticed Tekos, who stood some distance away, smoldering in the sunshine. "Who is that, Aia?"

"That is Tekos of the Belli," she said. "He saw the star strike their capital. He led me through the fire surrounding Sekaiza and brought me to the pit of the fallen god."

"When I look at him, I see a raging fire," said Caros.

Aia glanced at Hilerno, who looked as if he wanted to kill Tekos. She wondered who would win if they fought. It seemed that the fire consuming his lands had somehow entered Tekos. As she thought of the countryside to the south, an idea came to mind. "Let's take most of our warriors and ride down to Orosiz. Tekos has told me of a secret road through the mountains. We can strike Contebacom Bel, and even Salduie itself."

"Always running away from a fight," grumbled Caros. "Have you no honor? Their warriors are before us. All we need do is wait for them to approach."

"No. It is a good plan," spoke Hilerno. "I shall lead the army through the hidden pass."

Caros shook his head. "Strike the Sedetani capital? It will take too long. Once we depart they will sweep through Numantia and will attack Arcailicos."

Aia drew the sword of Auruningica and held it aloft. "This blade shall bring us to them swiftly."

For a moment, they all stood transfixed by the beauty of the sword.

Aia put the blade away. "Hilerno should remain here."

"Brilliant." Caros smiled at Hilerno. "You are our best. They will fear to strike here with you standing before them."

Hilerno crossed his arms. "You deny me the honor of leading our people?"

"If the Arevaci go to war," said Caros, "I shall lead."

Hilerno obviously didn't like the idea, but he relented. "You are the king."

Caros gave Aia a stern look. "Perhaps you will learn to fight with honor after all."

* * *

Sunlight glittered off the ranks of the Arevaci war bands, who lined up on the field below Numantia. Warriors from Termesos stood with spears and tall red shields. Chariots from the towns Kolounioku and Voluce waited in the vanguard, their green and yellow banners, adorned with a white horse. Arriving from the towns which Hilerno had overcome, Sekobirikes and Rauda, strong bands of warriors stood ready to march south. Archers from Ocilis, Tucris, and Lutia wore blue tunics. At the head of them all stood the chariots from Arcailicos, where the king rode. Aia stood in a chariot pulled by white horses. Her chariot was painted white and was adorned with purple bougainvillea flowers, pink lantana flowers and white carnations. Tekos wore a gold Celtic helmet with cheek guards and carried a golden spear.

King Caros stood in front of a standing stone on a hill overlooking Numantia, which served as an oath-stone. Over a white tunic trimmed in blue, he wore a round steel breastplate. His gold Celtic helmet was decorated with trefoils and painted in red and blue. Caros carried a long Celtic sword, a Falcata sword and a spear with a steel, leaf-shaped blade.

The wind was still, as the world listened. Aia heard her father's oath from her chariot. "I, King Caros of the Arevaci, pledge to stop King Culchas of the barbaric Sedetani. I will stop them from tearing down our homes. I will stop them from raping our women and murdering our children. I swear by The Three Mothers who guard our people and I swear by Epona, who shall make our horses swift and strong. If I break my oath, let the sky fall upon me, let the sea rise up and drown me, and let the earth crack open to swallow me."

The wind came on. Tiny yellow flowers fell out of the trees, covering the green road with a carpet of gold. Caros got into his chariot next to his driver Kalos and his shield bearer Sigilo. Caros nodded, and Aia drew her sword. Sunlight shone down upon them both. Aia motioned with her sword for them to advance. The war bands of the Arevaci began their journey south. Aia listened to the warriors sing as they marched. Caros grinned. "Warfare is like a dance, Aia. Our journey south begins."

* * *

Music meandered through the great hall of Arcailicos. Aia wandered through the crowds, searching. She wore a long dress and a crown of flowers. Hilerno came over, stepping in her way. "Dance with me, Aia."

"No, thank you, Hilerno. I'm looking for someone."

"Two kings lay dead on separate fields of battle tonight. I stopped their aggression."

"Yes, it's a great victory," she said.

"I am the greatest warrior among our people," he grumbled. "But I'm not good enough for you, am I?"

"War can never make one great," she said.

Hilerno's gaze turned hot. "Yes it can, princess."

Beyond Hilerno, she spotted a group of the Lusones people, but Prince Karbelos was not among them.

"This celebration is in my honor," he said. "You belong at my side tonight."

"I'm sorry, but I can't."

"Is it because your father has already given your hand to another?"

Aia didn't answer. She slipped away through the crowd and rushed into the night. The courtyard was unoccupied. Leaning against a tree, she listened to the music while looking up into the River of Heaven. After a time, a voice broke into her reverie.

"Shall we dance, princess?"

Karbelos stood before her, dressed all in leather. A smile came to her lips. Aia let him carry her away in a whirlwind. They swirled round and round the courtyard. Alone and together, they danced among the stars.

* * *

White mists covered the green hills and orchards on the sides of the road leading east out of Titiacos. The Arevaci had crossed over the Salo River. The sun had just come up and cold light glittered off the spears and helmets of the warriors. Aia stepped into her chariot next to Tekos, surveying their strength.

Caros rode up on a horse, accompanied by a bodyguard of

men, all dressed in white. His face was determined, but he had a trace of wonderment in his eyes. "It has only taken a single day to travel here. In my youth, I traveled from Numantia to Titiacos and it took me four days. The goddess Epona is with us, daughter. At this rate we'll reach Salduie quickly."

They looked out onto the host of warriors assembled behind them. The size of their army had grown today. The Belli and Titti tribes had joined them in their march south. "I didn't expect the Belli and the Titti tribes to join us. What did you say to them, Aia?"

Aia gave her father a sidelong glance, holding back a smile. She shrugged innocently. "Why wouldn't they want to fight? They're our friends and allies."

King Caros seemed satisfied with her answer, and he rode away.

Tekos gave Aia an incriminating look. "You told them that we'd already destroyed half of Culchas' army."

Nescato, who rode behind their chariot, giggled. "They actually believed you."

Aia gave a sly smile. "I told them that sometimes, it's better to abandon one's self to destiny."

"You shouldn't use them so," Tekos muttered.

"The Sedetani are threatening their lands too." Aia's voice was calm, resolute.

Tekos would not back down. "Lying is not honorable."

"Honor is for fools," Nescato scoffed.

"Enough arguing," said Aia. "We need to get moving."

Tekos relented. "To get around the pit of fire, we need to go through Arcobis, but we will save time if we avoid the town of Bilbiliz. We will cross the Siloca River at Orosiz and then double back north to the mountain pass."

"Why, thank you, Tekos." Aia drew her sword, catching the

morning light.

Horns sounded, indicating an advance.

The men of the Arevaci went forth to war.

* * *

The songs died out when they came to the charred lands. All morning, a plain of ash stretched out before them. Great smokey clouds of ash swept into the air as they trudged through the blasted hills and plains that once held life. They were unable to forage for food, and Aia was glad they'd prepared for the journey, and that it went so quickly. Occasionally, they came to a burnt out village or the charred remains of people who'd been caught in the firestorm. The fires had died out completely, but the world was awash in smoke and ash that lingered in the nose and mouth. After a time, all of their possessions smelled like ash. They all wondered at the god who had fallen out of heaven, and looked at the desolation he had brought.

By noon the charred region gave way to life once again. King-fishers and other waterfowl flew over the river, and Aia spotted an eagle. Wildflowers grew along the road. Orosiz was full of throngs of people who'd fled the fires burning out of the north. Sosian, the lord of the town, allowed their army pass over the bridge without incident. Caros gave them food and blankets and promised to send more once the war had been won. Thickets of poplar, willow, and walnut trees gave plenty of shade along the sides of the road where they turned back north.

The Siloca River danced on the left side of the army as they marched. The warriors had begun to sing again and their music filled Aia's heart with joy. She felt a kinship with the eagle she'd seen soaring into blue skies. The mountains looked down upon them from the east, and as they traveled she felt as if they were being watched by whatever lurked in the darkness among the mountain peaks. Nescato grumbled about it, but Aia didn't care. "Let the Sedetani stop us, if they can," she said.

Eventually they came to the burned out region once again, but they traversed the area quickly and found themselves at the trail leading up into the mountains. They passed through the high places with steep cliffs on either side of the army, who had grown silent. After a short while, they came out on the other side of the mountains and looked down onto the plains that led to the Sedetani capital of Salduie. The king drew up his forces in sight of the Sedetani town of Contebacom Bel which stood in their path. They made camp the night of the fourth day out from Numantia.

Blue mists seeped out of the earth while the morning sun warmed the plains. The gates of Contebacom Bel were shut, the defenders silent. The host of the Arevaci were drawn up before the town, resplendent in their war banners.

Aia stood in her tent while her attendants, a girl named Stena and a young warrior named Liteno, arrayed and girded her for battle. Unaccustomed to armor, Aia wore leather and animal skins. Stena placed steel bands on her arms and a gold torc on her neck. Liteno brought over a finely woven cloak. Upon Aia's long, golden fair-tressed hair, Stena crowned her head with summer flowers. The sword of Auruningica was sheathed in a scabbard over her back and she had a short Celtic sword at her side.

Aia walked up to her chariot where Tekos waited. "Where is Nescato?"

"We're riding into battle, princess." Tekos got in and made ready to leave.

"Oh," she said. Aia had forgotten that Nescato was only a rogue and not a warrior.

King Caros stood among the leaders of the war bands. "In the past, we have always given prizes to the fiercest warriors. Today, I shall give awards for courageous restraint. Do not kill anyone except warriors and if they offer to surrender, disarm them."

The fire in Tekos seemed to ignite Aia's spirit. "No mercy," she declared. "I'd like to kill anyone with mercy in his heart today."

Tekos looked into her eyes. "How can you say that? We should offer quarter and take prisoners." He had changed. In the past, Tekos would have killed them all too. The fires in his heart had turned to ash.

"They have given no quarter to anyone they have fought. You more than anyone else should know that," she said. "Why should we offer it to them?"

"There is no honor in killing the weak and helpless," said Tekos.

Aia crossed her arms. "They would never treat me as I would want to be treated. They are a ruthless enemy, without heart, without soul."

Tekos was unconvinced. "Will you have a soul after you kill them all?"

"You can't fight the Sedetani without losing your soul."

King Caros ordered them to bypass Contebacom Bel.

Aia watched the silent town as they went by it. No activity at all could be seen in the fortress, but she knew the Sedetani living there were filled with a great relief. A contingent of warriors surrounded Contebacom Bel while the rest of the army rode past.

In time they came to the plains of Salduie that stretched out before the capital. King Caros rode up to Aia. "We have done well, daughter. The city is open to us. They are completely defenseless. Now, I will send a courier to the city and ask for their surrender."

Aia could no longer contain the fire in her heart. "How can you say that? We need to kill everyone in Salduie. All you need to do is to give the order to advance."

"Do not try to manipulate me like you've done to others. When Prince Karbelos—"

"I won't hear it!" Aia was shocked when she heard the name and she refused to let him finish. "If you don't kill them all, their children will grow up hating us and then they will come to kill us."

"What next? Massacres, mass executions, the maltreatment and murder of prisoners?" Her father's face was filled with sorrow. "I can't do it, Aia. Not everyone there is responsible for the evil they have done."

"It is noble to be kind and fight with honor," Aia said, "but our enemy is merciless and sadistic. You haven't seen the evil they have done."

"What kind of world are you leading me to?" Caros wasn't angry. His tone was sad. "What kind of people will we become? If we are ruthless, we won't be any better than they are. What right do we have to live if we are not good people?"

Aia looked at her father. "We will be alive and they will be dead."

The king did not give in. He sent a courier to the city. The host of the Arevaci waited in silence while the sun moved across the sky. After a long time, Aia looked at her father. "Your mercy might destroy us all."

"My mercy is what makes me a better man, a better king, than Culchas," said Caros.

It was late afternoon by the time the courier had returned. "They have refused to surrender, sire."

Caros nodded. "Very well."

Before Caros could give the command to advance, he was interrupted by the arrival of a rider on a swift horse. Aia recognized the long tresses of brown hair. The spy Saorla approached. In the distance, a large force of the Sedetani came up and spread out in front of their city. Saorla spoke, "King Culchas has brought his army down from Caiscata."

"We can see that," grumbled Tekos. Saorla looked at him and smiled.

"How did they get here at the same time as us?" wondered Caros.

"Culchas had a smaller distance to travel," explained Saorla.

"But how did they know we'd be here?" asked Aia.

Saorla glanced behind at the Sedetani army. "Lilura the Seer told Culchas of your arrival here on this day."

"If the enemy can predict what we'll do, how can we ever win?" Caros asked. "They also have the Magic Jar with the fallen god inside."

Aia drew her sword. "And we have steel."

"I bring more bad news, Lord Caros," said Saorla. "The Sedetani have besieged Numantia."

"What of Belexeia?" asked Aia.

Saorla's words were soft. "I do not know."

Silence mingled with sunshine.

"Culchas has sent forces to Titum," Saorla added. "They're under siege too."

Caros's face darkened. "All is lost then."

"No, it isn't," Aia replied firmly. "Let's defeat them. Now. Today."

Grim darkness turned to determination.

"Thank you, Saorla." The king nodded to his war leaders, who returned to their men. Caros placed a hand on Aia's shoulder. "Love has always abounded in your heart more than glory. Do not forget who you are, Aia."

With great noise and clamor, the Sedetani advanced in a great line. War bands armed with Falcata swords and tall shields formed their center behind a line of chariots while archers and spearmen deployed to either side. In the distance, Salduie stood in the sunshine, awaiting their fate.

Fear crept into Aia's heart at the sight of the Sedetani army. Taking deep breaths, she tried to shake it off, but the fear remained. Something else came too, alongside the fear: determination. She put a hand on her Tekos' shoulder. "Do not lift me up until I fall."

Tekos nodded, eyes fixed on the enemy line ahead.

The Arevaci warriors moved in silence, breathing in courage, ready to destroy their foes. King Caros made a sharp motion. A horn blared, and their chariots surged forward. Aia picked up a javelin while Tekos drove the horses. As they neared the enemy line, she heard a fierce shout and the Sedetani raised their shields. Aia threw her javelin, as did the other charioteers. They turned away from the enemy, circling around for another pass. Great swaths of the enemy fell down with each pass like wheat cut by a great scythe. Each time they circled around, more warriors filled in the gaps in their line. Aia ran out of javelins and signaled Tekos to return to the rear. All at once, arrows fell out of the sky, impaling their horses. The chariot flipped over, and Aia was thrown to the ground.

Aia lay on grass that was covered in wheel tracks, listening to the battle rage around her. She rolled onto her back and sat up. The chariot lay in ruins some distance away, dragged by the horses who now lay dying under the hot sun. There was no sign of Tekos. Aia stood up, bruised, scratched and disoriented but otherwise unharmed. Several other chariots had crashed, throwing broken men and horses onto the field. She called out, "Tekos!"

There was no reply.

Great clouds of dust swirled around the battlefield, thrown up by their chariots and by other warriors as they maneuvered. Like a tide washing in, a low rumble emerged out of the din of battle, growing louder and louder. Aia couldn't tell which way the sound was coming from. She drew her sword and grasped it with both hands. Slowly, she turned around in a circle, waiting for the enemy to appear.

All at once, a line of hundreds of chariots shot through the clouds of dust. One came at Aia and she had to jump out of the way to avoid getting trampled by the horses. Dodging javelins, she got up. One chariot shot past and she swung her sword, hoping to strike the rider but she missed. A loud crashing sound came from behind as the Sedetani chariots slammed into the Arevaci war bands. She could hear screams as men and animals died.

A steady march of boots approached from where the Sedetani chariots had come from. Aia saw a line of thousands of spearmen coming her way. Smiling, she readied her sword, refusing to run away this time. There was a whoosh, accompanied by hot winds and a trio of winged serpents, made entirely out of fire, swept by. They crashed into the Sedetani warriors, scattering the assault. A loud cry of the Arevaci swept over the battlefield, following the serpents into the fight. Aia saw Tekos standing by the ruins of their chariot, golden spear in one hand. Fire and smoke swirled around him. He pointed his spear at a line of Sedetani warriors and she saw one of the fire serpents swoop down on them, burning and killing. Aia heard the weapons of the Sedetani break as steel struck iron. Horns sounded in the distance and the Sedetani army retreated. Aia caught a glimpse of King Culchas in a chariot, fleeing south.

Aia walked over and stood next to Tekos. When he turned to

141

look at her, his eyes reflected the fires coming from the fire serpents. Sunlight glittered off his skin. He smiled when he saw her, but she took a step back. "Tekos?"

"We have won this battle with fire and steel."

"What are you?"

The fire serpents flew up into the sky and vanished. Fire and smoke faded away from Tekos as fatigue crept into his face. "I am—"

"You are a god."

"No," said Tekos. "I am—" He stumbled and had to lean onto the broken chariot wheel. "I am Tekos. I served under King Indortes, the ruler of the Belli tribes."

A hot wind blew through the battlefield. The air turned cold. Tekos looked disoriented.

Aia fingered her sword. "Who do you serve now?"

"I serve the fallen god," he whispered.

"Who do you serve?"

Tekos ran a hand through his hair, and shook his head. The fire faded from his eyes, like a candle going out. He straightened up and gave her a friendly smile. "I serve you, Aia."

Aia put her sword away.

Tekos looked out over the battlefield. The sun was going down and his strength went with it. "The Magic Jar is close."

"How can you know this?"

Tekos shrugged. "It calls out to me."

* * *

Nescato walked through the tribes of the Arevaci, which were illuminated by campfires. She led her horse, fully laden with treasures scrounged from the battlefield. She came to the largest tent and halted. Silence came from inside the king's tent. She patted her horse's mane. "Come, Iluna. Let us find our friends."

Nescato walked into darkness.

Inside the tent, King Caros lay upon a bed of animal skins, surrounded by warriors. A large bandage, stained in blood, was wrapped around his chest. Aia sat next to him, holding her father's hand. Caros smiled weakly.

Aia wanted to sink into the ground and let the earth cover her up. "I'm so sorry I brought you into this war, father. I have failed you."

"No you haven't," he said. "It was glorious, leading my people into war."

"I thought you were too weak to fight," she whispered.

"Do not mistake kindness with weakness, Aia," he said. "You will find that kindness takes more strength than cruelty, which is easy."

Aia looked away into the shadows. "What of glory? All I feel is emptiness, and shame."

Caros smiled. "Glory is how we become like the gods. Soon, I shall be fulfilled as a great warrior king, my most glorious moment. I only wish it had occurred on the battlefield."

Caros squeezed her hand. For a long time, they looked at one another, father and daughter, swimming in love. After a time, she realized that he did not want to let go of her hand. Aia held back tears, covering her face in a smile. "I need to go, father. I want to wipe off my face so that you can see me without the stain of battle. I want you to remember me as I was, the Princess of Flowers."

Caros nodded and let go of her hand.

Aia stood up. "I shall return shortly."

"I will wait for you," said Caros.

Aia stepped out of the tent, eyes full of tears. "What have I done?"

Tekos walked over and put his hands on her shoulders. She calmed down. "Your father fought with great honor, Aia."

"Don't talk to me like that," she said. "He's still alive."

"His wounds are too severe," said Tekos. "He will last only a few more days."

Aia looked into the night, towards the Salduie. "You said it was close, did you?"

Tekos glanced over his shoulder. "Yes."

"Then Tyresius is here, too," she said. "I can't see him leaving it alone for long."

A cold wind blew out of the east. Strange mutterings and whispers came with it, along with the smell of blood and death from the battlefield. Figures moved in the darkness beyond the light of the fires.

"What's happening?" she wondered.

A scream pierced the darkness. Full of despair, it was utterly alone. As if in answer, another cry spilled into the night, followed by more and more. A rising tide of terror swept into the camp.

Aia called out to a guard by the king's tent. "Abartanban, take my father to a place of safety, beyond Contebacom Bel."

"I shall see that it is done, princess."

She looked at Tekos. "Come on."

They went to the edge of their encampment and found a host of evil spirits cutting through the warriors, murdering as they went. The host of the Arevaci retreated from an army of the dead.

Drawing her sword, Aia met one of the spirits as it came on. It was a Sedetani warrior, freshly dead. His helmet had been split open, revealing a gash in his head. He thrust a spear at Aia, and she jumped aside. Moving forward quickly, she stepped inside his guard, so that he couldn't use his spear. As he stepped back, she cut off his head and the body collapsed.

"Tyresius is here," she muttered.

Aia turned around and saw the entire host of the Arevaci scattering into the night like a flock of crows, pursued by the dead army.

Following the setting sun, victory faded away to defeat.

"No!"

Aia felt a blow to the back of her head and fell into darkness.

*　*　*

CHAPTER EIGHT

Belexeia's Secret

Cold stone pressed against Aia's cheek. A throbbing pain in her head reminded her that she was still alive. It was a cruel reminder of failure. Drums sounded from somewhere, accompanied by chanting and music, drifting back and forth like a bloody scythe of death. In the distance, screams interrupted the rhythm of the drums. Aia opened her eyes and passed from one nightmare into another.

She lay face down on the stone floor of a tower divided into separate cells by iron bars. Fading light fell into the room from a high window set in the stone wall. Her body was limp, her arms sprawled underneath her. With a groan, she rolled over into a beam of dazzling light that blinded her for an instant. She raised her arms to shield the brightness and found that her hands were bound together. She rolled to the side, out of the light, and a wave of pain swept into her head again, causing her to close her eyes against it.

Once again, she raised her hands and heard the clinking of

chains. She looked down to see that her wrists were bound in circlets of iron that were attached by a long chain to an iron ring affixed to the wall. Light glittered against gold along one side of the chamber. A stack of war trophies lay there, against the wall, carelessly discarded by someone who must have gathered more than they could carry. Her sword rested against her father's gold helmet. A package, wrapped in gray silk, lay there as well.

Aia got up to retrieve her sword, but the chains held her back. Swimming in agony, she dropped to her knees again, closing her eyes, as if the darkness could cover up the pain. Something warm dribbled down her forehead. The soft sound of clattering chains drilled the pain into her head even more as she lifted her hands to feel her head. When she looked down into her palms, they were covered in blood.

A melodic voice came out of the blackness from the other side of the room. "Alive? How sad."

Aia peered across the room. A woman sat with her back against the wall, her wrists bound in chains. Long brown hair fell into her face, obscuring it, but Aia recognized her. "Belexeia?"

"They'll torture you," said Belexeia, "and then they'll kill you."

"Where are we?"

"Does it matter, really?"

Aia sat down onto her heels. "I suppose not."

After a moment of silence, Belexeia asked, "Have you ever been to Iltiria?"

"No."

"It's a town beside a river that comes down from Mount Aneto, close to my home."

"Val d'Aran."

Belexeia nodded. "Yes. My father, Andereseni, was a merchant.

He heard of a new kind of tree they were growing in Iltiria. The wondrous tree produced a sweet golden fruit. The tree was brought out of the east by the Carthaginians. It was planted in the gardens of the king of Iltiria. My mother wouldn't let my father travel so far alone, so we all went along. My brother, little Cison, was so excited. It took us sixteen days to come down from the mountain. We arrived at Iltiria and my father found the tree. It had pretty white blossoms and the fruit had a wonderful aroma. They called it a Narang Tree. My father purchased the golden fruit for us. Cison couldn't get enough of them. He ate a whole basketful."

Aia was curious. "What did it taste like?"

"Like sun shining on a meadow blooming with wildflowers."

In spite of the pain in her head, Aia smiled.

"Then the Sedetani came to Iltiria. The king would not submit. After Culchas took the town he burned down all of the Narang Trees. There was no need to, really. It was an act of cruelty."

Belexeia's voice faded into silence.

"They killed your family."

Belexeia nodded.

"How did you escape?"

"I jumped into the river and swam away."

"I'm sorry what they did to you, Belexeia." Aia wondered why Tyresius kept the girl locked in a cell. Was he afraid of her magic?

Belexeia changed the subject. "So you have been tossed into a room full of the spoils of war. You must be one of the prizes. Maybe they won't kill you."

"Tyresius thinks I am his."

"Why would he think that?"

"A gift, he said, from the fallen god."

Belexeia hissed. "The fallen god did not come here to give us

149

gifts."

Aia noticed that the silk package was within her grasp. She reached out for it.

"Keep away from that!"

Belexeia did not shout, but somehow, the soft words from Belexeia made the pain in Aia's head throb more intently. She winced. Aia threw her words back at her. "How can it matter what I touch now?"

Aia picked up the item and found that it was a large square of metallic silver, wrapped in gray Persian silk. Withdrawing the cloth, she saw that the silver tablet was inscribed with ancient arcane symbols. On the other side an incantation was written in blood:

By means of this magic tablet,
I call down the Mighty One from heaven,
To smite my enemy, the Sedetani;
To consume them with fire.
I beseech you, Lord Apollyon, to destroy them all.
Grind their bones into ash,
And scatter them into the wind.
That Salqiu may take their spirits to the underworld.
It is the fate of the defeated to which they shall be destined;
The center—when he sows it—shall be whole.
I right their wrongs blindly,
By means of this tablet I shall see what shall be.
By Lugus I prepare them;
By Lugus I prepare them;
By Lugus I prepare them.
By the light.

Gently, Aia put down the silver tablet and wrapped it back up in gray silk. She looked across the chamber at Belexeia, and a cold realization dawned upon her. "You called down a god from the heavens."

"I wanted to destroy them, to incinerate them with fire. So I created a magic square and brought down a god from the River of Heaven."

"The fireball landed on the Belli town of Sekaiza. Not Salduie."

"I don't know how that happened," said Belexeia. "Lilura must have anticipated—"

"Do you know how many people have died because of you?"

"I don't care!" Belexeia's shout was startling, but her next words chilled Aia to the bone. "Let the world burn."

Aia looked upon the dark face of a woman utterly consumed by hatred. She thought of her own struggles against Culchas. Was it truly Belexeia's fault that so many had died? Aia felt sorry for Belexeia. She was a slave to hatred and vengeance. It was like watching someone consumed in a raging fire. Aia wondered if she would ever be able to extinguish the fires in her own heart. If the fallen god had burned Salduie, where would Belexeia be now? Her face was full of hatred. What would it look like when it was empty?

The sound of a door opening scattered her thoughts into the darkness.

Soft footsteps approached— soft and deadly, like a mountain lion stalking prey. Aia looked up and saw King Culchas, accompanied by two men. One was a Sedetani warrior, the other was a Carthaginian. Culchas was covered in sweat and blood and dust from the road. He looked exhausted, but fire still burned in his eyes.

Culchas halted in front of her cage. For an instant, he stood frozen, awed by her beauty. Aia felt his eyes drift over her body, like the caresses of a serpent. She had an urge to cross her arms but remained still.

151

"So we meet again," said Culchas. "How does a thief such as you end up on a battlefield?"

"I am no thief."

Culchas gave her an incredulous look. "What are you, a warrior?"

"Yes."

Culchas chuckled. "Only those who devote their lives to making themselves powerful deserve the title of warrior."

"I am Aia, princess of the Arevaci," she said, "and I beat you on the field of battle."

He mocked her with a smile. "So here you sit, in your cage, victorious."

While Aia simmered in silence, Culchas made a motion to one of his warriors who opened the cage. Culchas stepped inside and went over to the pile of treasure. He picked up Aia's sword and took it out of the scabbard. His eyes were full of wonder. "Quite an exquisite blade," he murmured.

Culchas placed the sword's edge against Aia's throat. "Where did you steal it from?"

"I didn't steal it."

"No?" Culchas seemed tempted to strike her down. For an instant, she thought he would do so. She closed her eyes, but instead of a blow, he spoke again. "How did you come by it?"

"The goddess Epona led me to a glittering cave under the—"

"Tell me—how many lies does it take until you start believing in them yourself?" Culchas had withdrawn the sword from her throat.

Aia frowned. "Everyone had always believed me, until I started speaking the truth."

"So, that irritates you?" said Culchas. "You are completely

devoid of honor."

Aia looked away into the shadows.

Culchas glanced at Belexeia. "When Lilura stated that my greatest adversaries were two women, I didn't believe her."

"No?"

"Crazy talk from a Lusitanian Seer," he muttered. "I really don't know why Tyresius keeps her around. Lilura foretold that you would cause his death."

"She loves him," whispered Aia, "but he doesn't know it."

Culchas didn't respond. He glared at her in silence.

Aia looked up at him. "You don't care about anyone, do you?"

"Love is for the weak." After a moment of silence, he said, "You think that I am evil."

"Aren't you?"

His eyes drifted away. "I was a good person once. One day when I was a child, I heard the approach of warriors from the Illercavones tribe. They slew my mother. They slew my father and all of the rest of my people. Some of us survived the attack. We were forced into a life of slavery. My father died because of his weakness. The world destroys good men. So I concentrated on becoming the strongest person in the world. Finally, I broke free of my bonds and killed my masters. Then I raised up an army and conquered those who had enslaved me. The Illercavones were the first to fall under my sword."

Aia dropped her gaze and blonde hair fell into her eyes. She wondered if she should feel sorry for him. "Are the two of us really that dangerous?"

A cruel smile spread across his face. "Perhaps not."

Culchas motioned to the Carthaginian and pointed at Belexeia. "Gisco, kill her."

Aia tried rising to her knees but Culchas placed the sword back at her throat. She sank down onto her heels again.

Belexeia quietly looked at the warrior as he entered her cell. Grinning, Gisco drew his sword. He raised the blade and began to strike.

All of a sudden the warrior ignited into a pillar of flame. His screams sent chills down Aia's back. Culchas had an irritated look on his face. He motioned to the Sedetani warrior, who drew a sword and killed the Carthaginian.

Silence gradually settled over the prison. Aia stared at the smoldering remains of the warrior and she noticed smiling eyes under Belexeia's locks of hair. So that was why Culchas kept her in a cell. Stalemate. What spells had the Enchantress used to protect herself?

His eyes were as hot as the fire that came from the fallen god. "So King Caros of the Arevaci came here to fight me. Now his army is destroyed and he has fled into hiding. By what right do you wage war against us?"

"You invaded the lands of our friends, killed their people," said Aia. "You started this war and threatened to bring it to my people."

He laughed. "You seek retribution?"

Aia looked into his eyes. Steel met fire. "In warfare, one must always be on the side of justice."

"Warfare *is* justice," he said.

Culchas brought the blade up to Aia's chin, a silent reminder of his power. "Orisos was right," he muttered. "I should kill you."

"Where is the Lord of Massacres?"

"He sailed down the Iber River to retrieve my second army from Celsa. Now, Celtiberia will have to contend with my subjugated tribes, the Illergetes, the Laietani, the Ilercavones, the Edetani, and Carthaginian mercenaries."

"Why have you invaded Celtiberia?"

"How can you ask that after you've experienced the thrill of battle?" he said. "To grind my enemies into dust, to make them grovel beneath me, is what I live for. Conquest is all there is. It is who I am."

The idea of it made her skin crawl. But she'd sought the same thing. Her words were soft. "You seek greatness."

"Yes." Culchas tilted his head slightly, as if he was trying to read her mind. "You once said that I will never be great."

"That's right."

Culchas shook his head. "Goodness can never lead to greatness."

Aia looked away into the shadows. "I will never believe that."

"Strength leads to greatness," said Culchas, "and warfare makes us strong."

"Warfare is madness," said Belexeia. "All it leads to is suffering."

Both Aia and Culchas looked at the Enchantress in surprise. They had forgotten she was there, watching them argue about what it meant to be great.

Deciding to ignore the Enchantress, Culchas laughed out loud. "I shall build a Celtic empire to rival the Hellenes and the Carthaginians." Culchas grinned. "Women weaken the heart. That's how you lost."

"I beat you in battle," said Aia.

Culchas shrugged. "Yes. You slew my warriors, but Tyresius used the fallen god to raise them up again. You can't fight sorcery with kindness."

"Yes you can," whispered Aia. The response came out of nowhere. She said the words without thinking about them, but she instinctively knew she was right.

155

Culchas leaned close to Aia. "You know what your greatest weakness is?"

Aia raised her eyebrows.

"Curiosity," he said. "Curiosity is what brought you to the pit of fire. Curiosity is what brought you here. You want to know more about me. You want to learn what it takes to be a king, since your father is too weak to rule."

"You're not a real king. You're a thief." Aia dropped her eyes into the darkness, where shadows moved. "You think you can steal victory."

Culchas pressed the blade against her throat. "Victory is victory, no matter how it is achieved. I have won. Most of your people will now become Carthaginian slaves."

Aia had failed her people. She had failed her father. She lowered her head, hoping he would chop it off.

Culchas slid the sword back into its scabbard and tossed it onto the ground next to the other treasures. He laughed. "No. I shall keep you for myself. You are too beautiful to kill."

Culchas went out of the prison, chuckling.

Under her breath, she said, "Tyresius may have something to say about that."

Aia took a deep breath and was about to lay down onto the floor in defeat when she caught a glimpse of something moving in the shadows. She froze, staring at the dark corner in the hallway outside their cells.

Nescato emerged from the darkness. "I thought he'd never leave."

Aia and Belexeia smiled at Nescato.

* * *

Timid sunshine hovered over pools of shadows by the wall.

156

Nescato led them down a narrow street that passed under the fortress. Aia was starting to think that they'd be able to move about unnoticed, until the three women passed by a group of Sedetani soldiers. One of the men whistled. Rather than try to avoid them, Aia walked directly up to a soldier with long dark hair.

She spoke Iberian, "Pardon me, but can you tell me which tower is the one where the Necromancer Tyresius is staying?"

The smile faded from his face. "That's no place for a beautiful woman."

"Oh but it is," she said. "I am his and he is mine. I am a gift from the fallen god. We all serve the fallen god."

The man turned pale. Rather than answer, he pointed at one of the towers attached to the fortress.

Aia smiled. "Thank you, kindly."

They walked by the soldiers, who had fallen silent. As soon as they were out of sight, Aia turned to Nescato. "What town is this? Are we in Salduie?"

"No," said Nescato. "This is Contebacom Bel."

Belexeia pointed to the gateway that led out of the town. "Shall we go?"

Aia shook her head. "I'm not leaving here without the Magic Jar."

Nescato and Belexeia exchanged glances. Nescato nodded. "Very well. Lead on."

A cold wind blew over the streets as they walked up to the necromancer's tower, which was unguarded. Aia wondered if the Sedetani soldiers were afraid to stand there. They entered and found a staircase that led upward. Belexeia held Nescato back. "Wait."

Nescato looked into Belexeia's eyes. "What is it?"

Belexeia's words were soft. "Dark forces seek to devour your soul."

Aia bit her lip. She'd forgotten to tell Nescato that Ataecina, Goddess of the Night, had called out her name at the battle of Contrebia Leukade.

The enchantress took an amulet from around her neck and put it on Nescato. "This will protect you from the Dark Queen."

"You should never have taken that amulet from Faiatura," complained Aia.

"I have no idea what you're going on about."

Nescato insisted on playing the innocent victim. She touched Faiatura's amulet and disappeared into the shadows. Aia thought she heard her friend going up the stairs, and Nescato whispered, "You coming?"

Drawing her sword, Aia went after her, followed by Belexeia.

Whispers emanated from a cold door made from iron at the top of the stairs. A nine-pointed star was scratched into the surface of the metal, along with a series of ancient symbols, like the ones covering the standing stones. She decided that the writing was probably an ancient Atlantean script. A large blue crystal sapphire had been embedded in the wood frame above the door. The sapphire glowed, lighting the hallway. Nescato appeared in front of the door, having let go of the amulet of Faiatura. She reached for the door handle.

"No," warned Aia, eyeing the door. Tilting her head, she considered. "Maybe we should find another way in."

"Why are we even considering it?" asked Belexeia. "Let's get out of this town."

Nescato grinned. "Where has your curiosity gone?"

Aia shuddered. "The last time I stepped into Tyresius's chamber, the Avatar of Neito put a sword through my stomach."

"This is a different place," said Nescato. "It may not even be

Tyresius' room."

"No," said Aia. "Tyresius is near. I can feel it."

Belexeia closed her eyes for a moment. "Spirits of the dead are near, too."

The whispers from beyond the door formed into words: "Come."

Aia stepped back, arching an eyebrow. "Did you hear that?"

Nescato frowned. "I thought I heard Tekos, just now, calling out."

"If only Tekos were here with us," Aia said under her breath. "Leave if you care to, Belexeia—but I'm not going back."

Changing her mind about being cautious, Aia opened the door and went into the room at the top of the tower. Nescato glanced at the blue sapphire, whose light had gone out as soon as the door had been opened. She exchanged glances with Belexeia, who shrugged and went inside. "Basajaun, protect me," muttered Nescato, and she stepped through the door.

Sunshine flooded into the room from a window that looked out onto the distant Iber River, where Salduie stood, enshrouded in mist. A large four-poster bed rested in the center of the room. The feather bed was covered with fine linen. A large bear-skin rug lay next to the bed and a sturdy wooden chest sat next to it. A large oval mirror was attached to the left wall. A thin, black mist seeped out of the glass like steam escaping from a cooking pot. Nescato approached the mirror, curious. A desk stood next to the door, and a large book lay open upon it, next to a pair of unlit candles. A cone of burning myrrh incense on the desk filled the room with a sweet fragrance. Next to the window, the Magic Jar sat, bathed in sunlight, beside a curtained alcove. Drums beat out a steady pace from down in Contebacom Bel.

Aia strode over to the Magic Jar.

Belexeia screamed.

Aia spun around and saw a black misty arm protruding from the mirror. A clawed hand gripped Nescato by the throat. Before Aia could react, Nescato grabbed the amulet Belexeia had given her. A shriek came out of the glass. The arm released Nescato and retreated back into the mirror, which shattered into a thousand pieces. Nescato dropped to her knees, clutching her neck.

The curtain covering the alcove parted and the Avatar of Neito stepped out into the room. He drew his sword and tried to strike Aia in the head. Aia ducked out of the way and drew her sword, just in time to block another strike. The Avatar continued with a series of strikes, and Aia parried them, retreating until she was against the stone wall. Grinning, the Avatar aimed a massive blow at the top of her head. Aia raised the Sword of Auruningica to block it and the Avatar of Neito's sword broke. Aia stabbed him in the chest before he could react. Falling to his knees, the Avatar gripped his chest. Aia beheaded him with one swift stroke. She looked at her sword in wonder. "Truly, this is the weapon of a goddess."

Belexeia helped Nescato to her feet.

Aia retrieved the Magic Jar. As she touched it, all of the pain in her head went away. She grinned. "Let's away."

* * *

White mist blanketed the slopes leading up into the mountains to the west of Contebacom Bel to mingle with the morning light. Though it was summer, the heat of the day had not yet touched the world. It was cold. The fires on the other side of the mountains had gone out, littering the sky with dirty ash. Aia and her friends rested in a ravine where a stream came down from the mountains. Nescato stood in the water, her boots left on a nearby rock. They

160

were exhausted and hungry.

Aia surveyed the mountains.

Nescato grumbled, "We're in a maze of twisty little gullies, all alike."

"Always the complainer," mumbled Aia.

Nescato shouted at Belexeia, "Why don't you try conjuring up a fish?"

"I'm an Enchantress, not a Conjurer," said Belexeia.

"I thought it would be easy to find the mountain passage," said Aia. "After all, we just brought our army through it."

Nescato called out, "That's why it's called a 'hidden pass.'"

"Well, perhaps Tyresius won't be able to find it either," said Aia. She wondered what he would do with his army of the dead. Would he use it to invade Celtiberia? She looked at the Magic Jar, which rested on a tuft of grass. A rustling sound, like leaves blowing across a field, whispered from the amphora jar. It was caught up by the morning breeze, and was carried out onto the plains. The rustling noises made her nervous. Was it calling out to Culchas?

"What a fine rescue," said Aia. "I should think you would know where you were going."

"Want me to bring you back to the Sedetani fortress?" asked Nescato.

Belexeia smiled at their bickering.

"What are you grinning at?" asked Aia.

Belexeia closed her eyes and leaned against a rock. "All will be well," she said. "We have the fallen god."

"Not if they catch us," whispered Aia.

Hoof beats, accompanied by the sounds of turning wheels, approached the mouth of the gully where they'd hidden for the night. Nescato gingerly moved over to her boots and put them on while Aia drew a sword to face the intruder.

A gust of wind came on and the clouds swept into the east. As the lone chariot rode into view, a burst of sunshine surrounded it. Pale smoke drifted from the backs of the white horses pulling the chariot. Bathed in sunlight, the driver stood up and raised a golden spear.

Aia put her sword away. "Tekos!"

"All of the Sedetani army are looking for us, along with a host of spirits of the dead." Nescato put her hands on her hips. "How did you find us?"

Tekos did not approach. He pointed his spear at the Magic Jar.

Glancing over her shoulder, Aia thought she heard a whisper coming from the fallen god. Picking up the Magic Jar, she walked over to the chariot and got in, followed by the other two. "Take me to my father."

* * *

The remnants of the Arevaci host were encamped high up in the mountains, through the hidden pass that led over the peaks. Hundreds of tents stood in the fading light of the day. Tekos drove his chariot into the camp and halted in front of the king's tent. Saorla, who was standing outside next to a fire pit, had a surprised look on her face. Aia picked up the Magic Jar, stepped out of the chariot and walked towards the tent entrance, only to be stopped by two sentries barring the way with their crossed spears.

"What is this?" she demanded.

"The tribal leaders have ordered that no visitors are allowed entry, princess."

"My father is near death, is he not?"

"Yes," replied the guard. "I'm very sorry."

"What will I become once he is gone?"

162

"You shall be our queen," he replied.

"Then I order you to let me through."

The pair of soldiers exchanged nervous glances. "Yes, my queen." They withdrew their spears, allowing her to go in.

"Don't call me that," she grumbled as she entered the tent.

King Caros lay on a bed, silent. A bronze brazier had a fire going, which threw light and warmth into the tent. Incense burned, too. Several leaders of the surviving war bands were also in attendance. The Druid Piresso sat next to the king. He was as surprised to see her as she was to see him. "Princess Aia, it is good to see you."

Aia walked up to the bed and placed the Magic Jar onto the floor. "I heard that you had been banished, Piresso."

"Yes, it is true," he said, "but the king rescinded his order when he marched into battle." Piresso gave her an intense look. "The burden of command has come to you."

Afraid her words could make it come true, Aia whispered, "I have no desire to be queen."

Piresso put his hand on her shoulder. "Yet it is the fate which confronts you."

Aia could hear her heart beating and she shivered against the cold. Fear gripped her soul. All she wanted was to destroy the Sedetani, to tear down their towns, to slay them all. Like drinking out of a cask of ale until it was impossible to reason, Aia stumbled into a world where all of the kindness in her heart would eventually fade away. Goodness would become no more than a shadow of her past. "They used to call me the Princess of Flowers."

Piresso smiled. "Yes. Many have enjoyed the gardens you have planted."

"I shall become a cruel tyrant when I am queen."

"The choice is yours," he said. "It is upon you now."

In a distracted tone, she asked, "Has anyone heard from Hilerno?"

Caciro, the ruler of Kolounioku, said, "Numantia still stands, but Hilerno fell in battle."

Though Aia did not like him, she knew that Hilerno was their best general. She took her father's hand into hers. He did not stir when she did so. She leaned forward and whispered in his ear, "Don't leave me, father." Aia held back tears. "I don't know what to do without you."

Caros was silent.

Aia moved her father's hand over to the Magic Jar and placed it there.

Nothing happened.

The others looked on, curiously. Caciro asked, "What is this?"

"The god which fell out of the River of Heaven has been imprisoned inside this Magic Jar." Aia shook her head, bewildered. "Why will you not heal him?"

Piresso placed his hands on Aia's shoulders. "Princess, there is no power which can—"

"No." Aia threw his hands off her shoulders. She looked at the Magic Jar. "All of the blessings of humanity are contained inside, that's what Lilura had said."

Caciro interjected, "Princess, perhaps—"

"No!" Aia stood up. "All of you, get out!"

The war leaders stood still.

"Out, out, out!"

Caciro said, "Very well. I have many wounded men to attend to."

The others went out too. Piresso gave Aia a sympathetic glance just before he left.

Aia knelt down besides her father. "No, no, no," she whispered. "You can't leave me!"

A murmur emanated from the Magic Jar.

Aia glared at it. "What do you want?"

The murmur turned into a whisper, "Release me."

Aia stood up.

The whisper returned, wreathed in fire: "Release me!"

Tyresius had told Lilura that he had imprisoned the fallen god inside the amphora jar to prevent him from destroying the world in a divine firestorm. Aia backed up. "I can't."

Murmurs turned into a grumbling rumble, like fire crackling in a pit.

A groan escaped from her father's lips and his hand slipped down to the floor.

"No!" Aia leapt forward, taking her father's hands into hers again. She placed it onto the Magic Jar. "Why is it that everyone who touches you has their wish granted, but I am denied?"

"What is your wish?"

The voice came from Tekos, who stood behind her. Fire smoldered in his eyes, a raging conflagration waiting for a spark to ignite into a new firestorm. For a moment, Aia was disoriented. She did not hear him come in. Tekos had a strange look, as if he was inside a waking dream. He repeated the question. "What is your wish?"

Aia brushed a strand of hair out of her face and looked into his eyes. "Heal my father."

"Speak the name of the fallen god and he will obey."

"His name?" Aia had no idea what it could be.

As if he had been called away, Tekos went back outside of the tent.

Aia knelt down on the floor next to her father. She took his

165

hand up into hers and bowed her head, defeated.

The whisper returned, "Release me."

"No!"

Aia closed her eyes and listened to her father's shallow breathing. Time passed, and her mind drifted away, back to her time as a
young maiden planting flowers in Arcailicos, to the start of the war.
She remembered seeing the fallen god as he fell out of the River of
Heaven, and how she had undertaken a quest to find it. Her mind
finally drifted back into the prison cell where she had found the
magic square which Belexeia had used to call down the fallen god.

Aia opened her eyes and looked at the Magic Jar.

"Apollyon," she whispered. "That is your name."

She stood up, her voice steady and commanding. "Apollyon, I
order you to heal my father."

A whisper, "So it shall be."

The inside of the tent was bathed in light. Aia heard her father
gasp and his breathing returned to normal. A moment after, he sat
up straight and smiled. "Aia, it is good to see you."

Aia gave him a long hug and, rather than let him see her tears,
she went outside.

Tekos stood at his chariot, feeding his horses. Saorla stood next
to him, awkwardly trying to think of something to say. Aia ran up
to Tekos, threw her arms around him and kissed him passionately
on the lips. To her surprise, he kissed her back.

Out of the corner of her eye, Aia noticed Saorla's angry, jealous
gaze.

Aia didn't care.

*　*　*

CHAPTER NINE
Into the Fog

Rows and rows of injured and dying warriors lay on beds under a large tent at the center of the Arevaci camp. The coppery smell of blood filled the air. Cries of pain and despair drifted up into the sky where an immense flock of sacred birds circled. Aia held the Magic Jar under one arm and walked into the center of the tent. Placing it on the ground, she whispered, "Apollyon, I command you to heal all of these warriors."

An irritated hiss escaped from the amphora jar, like steam escaping from a kettle of boiling water. A steady thrum thrum thrumming filled the air. Like a firestorm blown across a field of dry grass, a flash of warm light spread throughout the tent. A breeze of sweet perfume blew through the tent as if it had come out of a flower garden.

Stunned silence descended over all who lay there.

All of the men had been healed of their wounds. Some of them began to rise, astonished. All at once the tent was filled with excited talking, as if it were a crowded marketplace.

King Caros stood next to Aia, nodding his head in appreciation. "I am sorry I doubted you, Aia. The fallen god truly is powerful. Now we can—"

"No." Shaking her head, Aia had stopped him. "Our people have suffered enough. I've caused enough pain. Take our people back home."

"What of the war?" he asked.

Aia lied, "Culchas has no army, except those of the dead. Who knows how long they will follow him?"

"An army of the dead is a terrifying thought," he said.

Caciro walked over, his face full of wonder. He knelt down in front of the king. "I am glad to see you well, sire."

King Caros smiled. "Get up, Caciro."

As Caciro stood, Piresso walked up, a smile on his face. "Lord, all of our men seem to have recovered. It's a miracle."

Aia glanced at the amphora jar. "Thank the fallen god, Piresso."

Caciro gave the Magic Jar a wary glance. "What shall we do now, sire?"

Before the king could respond, Aia spoke, "Take our war bands back home through the hidden pass. We need to defend Arcailicos from those who have attacked Numantia."

They both gave her a suspicious look.

Aia laughed. "Why are you both looking at me like that?"

"I know you too well, daughter," said Caros. "You want to run away again."

"We have destroyed the Sedetani army," said Aia, "and we have the Magic Jar."

Caros and Piresso exchanged glances. After a moment, Caros

sighed and nodded his head. Turning to Caciro, he said, "Gather all of our men and make ready to move out at once."

Caciro saluted and went off into the encampment.

Piresso gave the king a curious look. "Will we strike the Sedetani capital?"

"No," said Caros. "Let them remember that we were here and chose to give them mercy. We shall return to Arcailicos."

After they went off, Aia allowed a slight smile to slip across her face.

* * *

Night had come. Almost all of the Arevaci war bands had marched through the hidden pass on their way home. The remaining army was still quite large and it had taken the rest of the day for them to get moving through the narrow pass. A chilly wind drew off the heat of the summer day and cold descended over the deserted campgrounds.

Aia stood by her chariot where Tekos waited next to the Magic Jar. Nescato and Belexeia both stood by their horses. Nescato had acquired a second horse to carry the plunder she had gathered from the battlefield.

"No more stupid quests for glory," said Nescato. She patted the draft horse on the neck and made sure the bags were secure. "I'm glad that you've finally grown tired of fighting, Aia."

The princess turned innocent eyes towards her companion. "Yes, I am quite weary."

Belexeia smiled.

As the last band of warriors, the rear guard of the Arevaci army, moved off into the darkness, Tekos gave Aia an expectant look. Aia got in and pointed in the opposite direction, back towards the Sedetani capital. Tekos turned the chariot around.

Nescato was shocked. "No, no, no, no, no. You can't!"

"Yes. I can," said Aia. "I will."

"But what about the army of the dead?" Nescato asked.

Aia didn't answer.

Nescato shook her head. "I thought you were practical."

Aia made a face. "Don't call me that."

"It's what you are," said Nescato.

"Not anymore." Aia's voice was soft. "I no longer wish to live with shame and dishonor."

Nescato crossed her arms. "I never noticed it bothering you."

"It has always bothered me."

Nescato sighed audibly. "Why do I keep following you?"

Tekos smiled. "I thought you were following me."

Belexeia got onto her horse. "You should take your plunder and go with the Arevaci."

Nescato wrinkled her nose and got onto her horse. "Face her father's wrath when he finds out? No way. I'd rather follow crazy suicidal people."

Aia smiled and tapped Tekos on the shoulder. "Away!"

* * *

They traveled toward Salduie for the entire day, always on the alert for Sedetani war bands or spirits of the dead, but the lands were silent, except for an occasional rabbit or deer. Aia caught sight of an eagle in the sky when they neared the Sedetani town, and thought it a good omen. She knew the journey would normally have taken them two or three days, and she marveled at the power of the magic sword on her back. For a moment, she wondered if she had made a terrible mistake. Her father would take a long time to return home, and by the time they arrived, Numantia could have fallen. Arcailicos might even be under siege.

They came to a hill covered with dandelions, overlooking the Iber River. To the northwest, the town of Salduie lay dreaming in the fading twilight. Aia realized that they were south of the battlefield where they had fought the Sedetani only a few days before.

Nescato fingered her amulet. "How is it that Queen Faiatura and the goddess Ataecina are both looking for me?" Her horse whinnied, perhaps sensing her nervousness. Nescato ran a hand along the mare's neck. "Easy Iluna."

"Now I know why she came with us," muttered Tekos. "Why else risk her plunder? She needs our protection."

"You are sworn to serve me too, Tekos, not just Aia."

Tekos chuckled. "Yes. Do not worry."

Nescato's horse raised her head and flicked her ears.

"What is it, Iluna?"

The mare snorted. Nescato's draft horse also grew nervous. The two horses pulling the chariot were calm, but they flicked their ears nervously. One of them snorted.

A rustling sound swept over the plain as if there were a steady breeze, but the wind was still. Down on the river, the surface of the water was smooth and quiet. The susurrations grew louder, and Aia felt a chill creeping down her spine. She turned all around, surveying their surroundings.

Suddenly, the draft horse neighed and ran off. Nescato's horse bucked in fear, throwing her to the ground. The mare ran off after the draft horse.

Belexeia looked down at their companion. "Are you all right?"

Nescato got up and dusted herself off. "I'm fine, though I don't understand why your horse is so calm."

Belexeia pointed towards a charm around her neck. Before she could speak, Nescato interrupted. "No, don't tell me what it is."

Nescato watched her horses running away into the fading light. "I'm going after them."

Tekos looked at her darkly. "If we have to leave, we can't wait for you."

After glaring at him for a moment, Nescato nodded and ran off across the plain.

Belexeia dismounted, stepped up to her horse and whispered something in his ear. She went over to kneel on a tuft of grass. She took out a bag of salt and poured it in a circle around the little rise. Placing a candle in the center of the circle, she began to sing softly.

Aia and Tekos got out of the chariot. While Tekos fed and watered the horses, she looked down at Salduie. Cooking fires began to light up the evening sky. Smoke rose into the air from hundreds of houses in the town. Her gaze wandered downriver to the water. A great fog was rising, pulled upwards by the fading summer heat which bled away when it grew dark. A distant neighing came from their rear. Aia turned around to see that Nescato was now completely out of sight. She grinned. "If I didn't know any better, I would think that the goddess Epona is leading poor Nescato away from us."

The rustling noise grew louder still. Aia had forgotten it, having gotten used to the sound for so long, but now she realized that it was no simple breeze. One of the murmurs turned into a anguished cry far off in the distance. A flurry of hundreds of little orbs of light rose out of the grass, sped up the hill and spun around them. All at once the grass surrounding their hill filled with rising corpses of the dead, having crept through the tall grass. The orbs materialized into wispy spirits. They were surrounded by the army of the dead. Aia drew the sword from the scabbard on her back. Tekos put down a bucket of water and picked up his golden spear. Belexeia remained where she was, rocking back and forth, singing softly. For the moment, the dead warriors did not approach.

A gust of cold wind came on, bringing some of the white dandelions with it. The flowers swirled around a spot not twenty feet from where they stood. A dark patch of smoke spun down from the sky and twirled into the figure of a man. Dark untamed hair framed shrewd eyes. Aia recognized the Lusitanean Necromancer in their midst. He carried the long spear of iron she had seen in the Dark Tower. It was covered with arcane silver symbols.

Tyresius smiled. "Ah, my gift has come back to me, and she has returned the fallen god."

Tekos stepped between them. Lowering his spear, he pointed it at the Necromancer.

The smile on Tyresius' face faded away. "Oh, yes, the Seraph imprisoned inside a man." Raising his spear, he shouted a command in the ancient Tartessian tongue. He plunged the base of his spear into the earth. A spark ignited there, and it produced many more, which danced across the grass.

Tekos cried out as a fiery conflagration burst around him. Bright light filled the hilltop. The man Tekos no longer stood there, having been replaced by a bright pillar of flame. Aia raised her hand to shield her eyes against the glare.

"Tell me," intoned Tyresius, "why you are here."

A voice emanated from the pillar of fire. "I am a guardian."

"Who are you protecting?" asked Tyresius.

"The fallen one."

"Bring the fallen one to me," commanded Tyresius.

The flaming Seraph moved towards the chariot where the Magic Jar was.

Aia darted towards the bucket and picking it up, tossed water into the air, drenching Tekos. A crackling hiss emanated from the flames and Tekos fell to the ground. The Seraph flickered a moment and faded away. Tekos lay unconscious with smoke drifting from his body.

Tyresius frowned. "What have you done, girl?"

Aia stood next to the Magic Jar. She blinked. "I—"

"Do you think it was your idea to travel here? The fallen god brought you. Indeed, you are lovely. You are the promised gift." Tyresius held out his hand, inviting. "Come."

Aia had always found the Necromancer darkly handsome. For an instant, she was tempted to join him. Her mind went back to the first time she had heard of him, when the king of the Sedetani had shouted his name. "I seem to remember Culchas warning you not to accept any gifts from the fallen god."

Tyresius thought for a moment before answering. "Yes. Culchas believes that a gift from the fallen god is an evil thing, a temptation for mortal men." He raised his eyebrows. "Are you evil, Aia?"

"Lilura seems to think so."

At the mention of the Seer, Tyresius grew silent.

Aia felt a weakness and thought to exploit it. "I am not yours. I came here to destroy the Magic Jar."

Tyresius laughed. "I have placed a Seal of Containment on the Magic Jar. It cannot be broken."

Aia raised the sword of Auruningica, thinking to strike the Magic Jar.

"Wait," Tyresius commanded.

Aia hesitated, curious.

"Do you know what it really contains?"

Aia raised an eyebrow. "You know his name?"

"No one knows the fallen god's name," he said.

In the distance, Aia noticed a fleet of warships sailing up the

Iber river. Orisos had arrived. She looked back at Tyresius. "Lilura said that it contains all of the blessings of humanity."

"It does," said Tyresius. "But it also contains a raging fire. Violence."

"What do you mean?"

Tyresius looked into her eyes. "On the floor of the palace of the gods stand two urns. The first urn contains all of the blessings of humanity. It contains peace of mind, sound health, labors of love, freedom from fear and worry, material riches, love and happiness. The second urn is full of evil gifts. Curses. It contains hatred, envy, jealousy, greed, fear, worry, indecision, doubt, ill health, frustration, discouragement, poverty and suffering. The gods send good gifts and evil ones to mankind—at a whim. So a person will sometimes meet with good fortune and at other times, bad. That is the way of things."

Aia glanced down at the Magic Jar. "I thought it contained the god which fell out of the River of Heaven."

"Do you know who the fallen god is?"

Aia shook her head.

"The fallen god is the one who delivers the gifts of the gods." Tyresius leaned on his spear. "His release will transform all humanity."

"How so?"

"Man will no longer remain subject to the impulses of the gods," said Tyresius. "Mankind shall be condemned to free choice."

"How can freedom be a bad thing?"

"We live in an age of violence. Warfare is part of our lives. Do not give the gift of choice to man over his fate. He will forever choose evil and his life will be full of suffering. It is best to respect the gods and pray for the good they might send us."

Tekos remained on the ground. Aia wondered if he was still alive. She glanced over at Belexeia, who was encircled by glowing candlelight. The dead took no notice of her, and Tyresius did not seem to be aware of the Enchantress.

Aia sighed audibly. "The gifts sent by the gods are full of sorrow."

"Yes," he said, "but the gods are kinder to us than we are to one another. True evil comes from mankind."

Aia tilted her head, suspicious. "What of the one who possesses the Magic Jar?"

Tyresius grinned. "The one with the Magic Jar shall gain all of the blessings of the gods and none of their evil gifts."

Aia lowered her sword. "You seek to cheat fate."

"I shall command my own destiny," he said.

"What of the rest?"

"Who?"

"Everyone else not sitting on one of your pillows."

"They are unimportant. They are as simple as sheep."

Aia raised her sword. "Then take it, if you can."

Enthusiasm faded from his face like a candle going out. Tyresius shook his head. He made a motion with his spear and the army of the dead came forward, inexorably, to retrieve the Magic Jar.

Aia cut several of them in two, kicked another one onto his back and beheaded some more. But they continued on, silently, swinging their weapons or throwing spears. Aia blocked all of their attacks and stepped out of the way of their spears. But she grew tired. After a time, she felt her legs knocked out from underneath and she fell onto her back. Cold hands gripped her underneath her arms and tried to drag her away. Aia rolled over, broke their hold and leapt towards the chariot where the Magic Jar stood. She looked down at the fallen god and spoke, "Apollyon, give me their souls."

All at once the army of the dead halted.

Tyresius dropped his spear. He stood with his mouth open as surprise lit up his face. His hands were shaking.

Aia stood up, catching her breath.

"No," he protested.

Pointing her sword at the Necromancer, she began to shout a command.

He shouted a word of command in an ancient tongue. Black smoke materialized and swirled around his body. It went up into the sky and climbed into darkness.

Tyresius had gone.

* * *

Orisos stood on the docks, broad-shouldered, lithe and strong as steel. He cradled his helmet in his arms and with penetrating eyes, looked on as his new army disembarked from the Carthaginian ships which had come up from the south. His face was burnt dark from exposure to the summer sun. Wild, blonde hair swept back from his forehead. To the north the Sedetani capital stood, brooding in the fading sunlight.

A courier rode down from Salduie and got off his horse in front of Orisos, who glared at the man, irritated. "Where is Culchas?" he asked.

The courier shrugged and handed the general a scroll.

Orisos broke open the seal and read it calmly. His eyes grew dark as his face filled with grim determination, but he smiled all the same. "At last," he muttered. Orisos stopped a passing warrior. "Bring me my horse."

Yellow sunlight spilled over the twisted trees that grew on the banks of the Iber river to the south of the dock. Dead things moved there. A flock of black birds ascended from the river, spooked by the creeping horrors that emerged from the reeds and bushes.

Aia rode in her chariot beside Tekos. She commanded of the army of the dead as it approached the Sedetani army. In her hands she carried a bladed polearm, a glaive made from Carpetani steel. The sword of Auruningica hung on her back and a short Celtic sword was at her side. Emerging from the river, the dead army approached the Sedetani army, which was obscured by the rising fog coming from the river.

Aia drew her sword and pointed it at the Sedetani warriors. "Destroy them," she shouted.

All of the dead advanced.

Tekos made a move but she put a hand on his shoulder.

"Wait."

The clash of iron and steel came out of the fog. A single scream of pain transformed into thousands more. The crash of breaking shields and crushed helmets grew louder. A nightmare crept over the warriors like an avalanche.

Aia smiled with grim satisfaction while listening to the death throes of the Sedetani army.

All at once, a group of horses sped out of the fog. Aia caught sight of Orisos on his black stallion, riding hard. She tapped Tekos on the shoulder. "Time to move."

Tekos spurred the horses into a run and the chariot swept towards the personal guard protecting Orisos. As they drew near, they were sighted and a group of horses broke off from the contingent to attack Aia. She picked up a javelin and threw it at the first rider, impaling him in the chest. One of the passing horsemen tried cutting her head off with a long Celtic sword, but she ducked out of the way. Tekos started to turn around to engage those who had gone by,

178

but Aia pointed forward. So he drove on towards Orisos. Looking over her shoulder, Aia noticed that they were moving at least twice as fast as any chariot could, and they quickly outdistanced their pursuers. So she directed her attention to Orisos.

Aia picked up another javelin and hurled it at the general. It struck his horse, who went down, throwing Orisos to the earth. Aia leapt out of the chariot and moved towards him. Orisos rose to his feet and drew a Falcata sword. Two of his guards rode forward. One aimed a spear at her chest while the second readied his long Celtic sword. She stepped to the side of the spear and sliced the second man's head off with her glaive. Though he was swifter, the bladed polearm had a longer reach than the second rider's sword. Aia turned around and barely missed a blow from Orisos by dodging to the side. Another horseman rode forward, and before she could engage Orisos, the rider got in the way, aiming a long mace at her head. She stepped to the side and avoided getting brained.

Orisos came on again, shouting a curse.

Aia had to dodge his strike and moved away a short distance. Another rider attacked out of the fog and she cut him in two. Turning around, Orisos was moving forward again, but this time she was able to use her polearm's reach to strike first. He parried the blow and ran inside her guard in a counterattack. Aia had to drop the glaive and leapt aside.

Out of the corner of her eye, she noticed Tekos fighting several horsemen with his golden spear. Small flaming serpents appeared and swept his enemies out of the way. Aia held back a smile and drew her sword to face Orisos.

He caught his breath and glared at her. "The only quality I respect in a warrior is toughness. Let's see if you're a warrior, or simply a dog to be put down."

Aia smiled. "Woof!"

Orisos leapt forward, swinging his sword at her head.

Aia parried it easily and stepped to the side again, rotating around, making sure that there were no others approaching. She held her sword out, pointing it at the general. The last glimmer of sunlight shone upon her and glinted off the sword of Auruningica. "Come on," she taunted. "Play with me."

Orisos yelled and attacked again, aiming a series of strikes at her, beginning with her head and then switching to her torso and legs. She parried all of his attacks and aimed a thrust at his chest, but he stepped out of the way.

He moved forward, delivering a series of strikes from different directions, one from above, another from below, another from the side, all aimed at different parts of her body. Aia retreated, parrying and dodging all of the attacks.

"Not very good," taunted Aia, "for the servant of the god of war."

His lips parted in a grim smile. "The gateway to paradise is under the shade of swords."

Hearing this made Aia wince at the memory of those he'd killed in the past. With a shout, she advanced, throwing a combination of sword strikes while moving in a circle around her quarry.

Orisos parried her strikes, and with one swift movement, knocked her sword out of her hand, disarming her. He laughed. "So, you are a dog."

Orisos aimed an attack at her head. Aia fell backwards onto the earth and he swung his sword down. She rolled out of the way as the blow struck the ground. Drawing her short sword, she swung upward, piercing his armor and finally striking home.

With a grunt of pain, Orisos fell down to the earth.

Aia got up and glared down at the dying man.

Moments later, Tekos returned to her. His eyes were full of fire, his enemies dead or burnt to ash. "The army of Orisos has been defeated and scattered," he said. "What now—princess?"

Aia looked at Salduie as the light of day went out.

* * *

Looking down at the town of Salduie, Aia smiled with grim satisfaction. She had arrived. Surrounded by an army of the dead ready to slay everyone in the town at her command, she was ready to do what was necessary to protect her people. With a glance down at the Magic Jar, which rested in the chariot besides her, she stepped out onto the grass. A lone bird called out and she heard the flutter of wings overhead. The moon was rising over the eastern mountains.

Coming out of darkness, Belexeia approached with a smile on her face. "Why hesitate?"

"Savoring the moment," said Aia. "That's all."

Tekos stepped out of the chariot and came over to where they overlooked the town. "You're making a mistake, princess."

Aia was surprised. "What?"

"To slay them all," he said, "is an evil deed."

"The Sedetani killed your king, murdered your people."

The fires in his eyes had gone out. "No." Tekos glanced over his shoulder at the Magic Jar. "The fallen god killed my people."

"So, I should let them live?"

"Yes."

"No!" shouted Belexeia. "The Sedetani are evil. They need to be stopped."

Aia thought back to the words of her father when he said that the Sedetani people were not responsible for what Culchas, their leader had done. Were their people truly evil?

"It is also wrong to keep them," said Tekos.

"Who?"

"The spirits of the dead," said Tekos. "These souls are trapped here now. Dead is all they know and death is all they deal in. Using someone in life is bad enough, but using the souls of the dead is an evil deed."

Belexeia hissed. "These souls burned our lands, killed our children, exterminated our people. Let them suffer for eternity."

Aia shook her head. "Where is Nescato?"

"You would seek the counsel of a rogue," grumbled Belexeia. She waved her arm at the town. "Destroy them all."

Movement from down by the river caught Aia's attention. It was a small child, running towards the town gate. A distant cry in the Iberian language drifted up to their position. "Mamma!" A woman stood at the gate, her arms outstretched. The child ran up and the mother picked up the child and rapidly went inside the town. A thumping sound in the distance signaled the closing of the gate. The Sedetani awaited their fate.

The words of her father came back. *Love has always abounded in you more than glory. Do not forget who you are.* A long sigh escaped Aia's lips. She walked over to the Magic Jar and put one hand upon it. Warm dreams entered her mind at the touch. Memories from long ago, when she had spent her time in the spring, planting flowers. When her father had nearly died, she was confronted with a question: What kind of queen would she become?

Aia's words were soft. "Apollyon, release all of these spirits so that they might find a place in the worlds beyond our own."

The dead fell down to the earth all around them, the strings that bound them no longer present. Ten thousand spheres of light, like tiny soap bubbles, drifted up from the corpses and found their way into another realm that bordered on the night.

An angry scream came from Belexeia. "No!"

The enchantress ran up to Aia and began striking out with her fists. "No, no, no!"

Aia grabbed her arms and held her away. "Stop it, Belexeia."

The enchantress looked into Aia's eyes. "There are those like me, who have lost the ones they love. They weep at their own helplessness."

Aia let go of her arms. "Look at what you have become."

Belexeia took a step back. Pain and sorrow lingered in her eyes, which filled up with tears. Her wail was one of the loneliest sounds Aia had ever heard. Belexeia turned around and ran away into the night.

Tekos and Aia looked at one another.

The words that came to Aia's lips were soft. "Help her."

Tekos nodded and went after the enchantress.

Aia walked over to the chariot and sat down next to the Magic Jar. She wondered aloud, "What next?"

The moon climbed high into the sky.

Galloping hoofbeats approached.

Aia stood up, but didn't draw her sword.

Saorla rode up and halted next to the chariot, followed by a cloud of dust. "Aia, I'm so glad to find you."

"What is it?"

"Culchas is hiding in a grove of trees next to the river." Saorla's voice dropped to a whisper. "He is alone."

Aia had wondered where Culchas had been throughout the battle. "Alone?"

"Yes," Saorla smiled. "Come."

Aia looked out into the darkness where Tekos had gone, half

183

expecting him to return with Belexeia in his arms.

Saorla was insistent. "I can lead you to him."

Aia's expression turned cold. "I may have shown mercy to the Sedetani, but there won't be any left for King Culchas."

She got into the chariot and followed Saorla into the glimmering darkness.

Moonlight filled the night with silver light. Saorla led them down to the river, along the banks past the Carthaginian fleet of warships, and up a slope. They reached a quiet clearing nestled in a grove of trees.

Saorla got off her horse and indicated that Aia do the same. They crept forwards through oak and fir trees, past jacaranda trees whose purple flowers glimmered in the moonlight. The sounds of the happy dance of a waterfall grew as they moved forward. They reached the edge of the clearing. Saorla motioned for Aia to wait.

A man lay by a pond near the bottom of the waterfall. His wild hair fell in tangles around his shoulders. His bare chest was covered in blood. There was a wild look in his eyes, which caught the moonlight. When Saorla went over to him, he laughed out loud.

"So soon?" he asked.

"I have brought you a horse, lord Culchas."

"Very well," he said. Culchas stood up.

Drawing her sword, Aia walked into the clearing.

Culchas froze in place and looked at Aia as she approached, with admiration in his eyes.

There was a smile on his lips. "Brilliant!"

Aia halted ten paces from Culchas. The sword of Auruningica glimmered in the moonlight. For a moment, they all stood still, listening to the sounds of the waterfall.

Culchas looked her up and down, obviously admiring her

beauty. "You are truly exquisite, thief."

"I'm not a—" the words caught in her throat.

Aia glanced around the silent clearing. Culchas laughed again.

"Why so mirthful?" she asked. "You are wounded and un-armed."

Culchas stood up straight "Do I look injured?" he asked. Culchas glanced down at the blood covering his body. "Oh, yes. This is the blood of my enemies, not mine."

Before she could respond, Culchas made a motion with his hand—a subtle flick of his fingers, almost dismissive.

For a heartbeat, nothing happened. Then the forest stirred. Leaves rustled, and shadows shifted between the trees. One by one, warriors stepped into view—silent, armored, and grim. Their blades caught the light in quick flashes, like teeth bared in warning.

Aia spun around, ready to fight them all.

She struck first, cutting a warrior down before he could react. Two of her adversaries moved in close, swinging Falcata swords at her and she leapt out of the way. Aia rotated around and caught a spearman who tried stabbing her in the back. She sliced off the tip of the wooden spear and then severed his head. Another pair of spearmen attacked and she tumbled out of the way.

Getting up, she blocked several spear thrusts, while turning to protect her back. A big burly man with a long Celtic sword advanced while trying to strike her in the head. Aia parried and lunged out, striking him in the chest.

For a moment, all of her adversaries remained where they were, at a distance. Aia faced down a wall of swords and spears. Out of the corner of her eye, she spotted a young warrior with a sling. He cast a stone at her, and it struck her head. Blackness touched her eyes, but she blinked it away.

Culchas laughed. "I do admire your courage, girl."

Aia shook her head to clear it, but before she could recover, strong arms grabbed her from behind, rendering her helpless.

Aia looked at Saorla in shock and surprise. "Why?"

Saorla smiled and brushed a strand of wild dark hair out of her eyes. Her words were a whisper, an invocation that came out of her deepest desires. "For Tekos, Aia. Tekos."

* * *

CHAPTER TEN
The Barbarian

It is not known what caused a god to fall from the skies or why he was cast out. Warfare among the gods is imitated by man, who is burdened with the lusts and passions that fill the hearts of all savages. Great things are won by taking great risks. So, with considerable effort, I brought the superior culture of the Hellenes to a dismal tribe of brutes scratching out a menial existence at the edge of the world. Sadly, the pitiable savages rejected me. I have come to realize that this failure is not mine. Inferiors are incapable of learning.

Princess Aia has become a violent barbarian. Perhaps slavery under the Carthaginians may one day help her, but I am doubtful she will ever embrace enlightenment. There are some among my people who capture wild animals and bring them back to Athens, with the hope of taming them, but they are usually forced to put down the poor beasts.

I weep for Gaia and all who dwell here, in perpetual warfare, a cycle of violence and depravity which may never end.
— *The Chronicles of Aristæus*

The great hall of Turiazu was filled with the aromas of a grand feast: roast beef, spiced ham, fresh bread, and hearty stews. Music and revelry filled the hall. Aia sat at the head table between King Olónico and his son, Karbelos. Hilerno sat brooding next to Queen Ana on the other side of the king, even as a trio of serving girls tried flirting with him.

Aia picked up a glass of wine and swirled it around while admiring the cup. "Such a beautiful thing," she said.

Karbelos smiled. "The merchant tells me that this glass came from as far away as Quart Hadasht, a Carthaginian colony on the coast of the great sea to the south. Civilization has brought us many great things."

The ripe cherry-colored wine had a hint of violet. Aia inhaled a nutty fragrance and closed her eyes as she took a sip. When she opened them again, she looked into the warm brown eyes of Karbelos.

"That man will spoil the party," grumbled Queen Ana.

A weary man entered the hall, carrying a satchel. Mud was on his boots. He approached the king, withdrew a scroll from his satchel and handed it to the king, who opened it.

A long sigh escaped the king's lips. "The Sedetani are bringing up a large force of warriors from the south. We will have to go out to meet them soon."

King Olónico began a conversation with Hilerno. Aia wondered if the general's advice would prove helpful.

Karbelos put his glass down.

"What is it, my love?" asked Aia.

"I do not wish to fight this battle."

"Why not?"

"The world has enough violence." A shadow passed through Karbelos's eyes. "War changes a man."

Aia was surprised at his timidity. She drank deeply from the cup of wine. It was a vintage from the south, where the Sedetani ruled. "I think it's a fine opportunity to win glory for your people."

Karbelos pushed his glass away. "I don't care about that."

"Don't you care about your people?"

"Of course I do."

"Then fight for them."

"Violence is a descending spiral which leads nowhere." Karbelos shook his head. "I thought you would understand that, Aia."

Aia called out to Hilerno, "General, will we bring a force here, as a token of our friendship?"

For the first time that night, Hilerno smiled. "Yes, princess."

Aia smiled back at him, letting her gaze linger a moment too long.

Hilerno got up and walked over. "Shall we dance, princess?"

"Yes, I like mighty men." Her next words were a whisper, intended for Karbelos. "Who is the greatest one of all?"

* * *

Aia stood on the deck of a Carthaginian bireme warship, sweating in the hot summer sun. Her hands were bound together. Two masts stood naked in the hot sun, their sails drawn up to the crossbeams high overhead. Aia stood near a ladder that descended into an opening on the wood deck. The aft of the ship held a large tent where King Culchas conferred with the ship's captain. The Magic Jar lay close to the king. The ship was propelled down the

Iber River by a hundred Carthaginian warriors who rowed to the beat of a drum.

A tall, pale-faced man wearing white and purple robes approached. As he drew near, Aia recognized that it was Baalhaan. He stopped a few paces away from her, face unreadable, voice as steady and cold as stone. "Welcome to the Melqart."

Not understanding, she raised her eyebrows.

"The Fire of Heaven," he said. "That's the name of my ship."

"Oh."

Baalhaan stepped back and examined Aia with a critical gaze. "Are you injured?"

Aia looked into his eyes, which were filled with casual indifference. She wondered if he was only being polite. "No."

Baalhaan let out a low, weary sigh, eyes lingering a moment longer on her before he turned away. He waved towards a passing sailor and called out in a cold, even voice, "You there."

The man halted and turned his attention to Baalhaan. "Yes, Captain?"

Baalhaan's nose twitched. "Clean her up, will you?"

The captain went away.

For a few minutes Aia wondered what had offended the Carthaginian, until a cold bucket of water was dumped over her head. She gasped as rough hands grabbed her shoulders and spun her around. A pair of bearded men stood in front of her and one of them thrust a cloth into her bound hands. Aia noticed a stream of bloody water flowing to the edge of the deck, through drainage holes in the side of the ship and out to the river.

A harsh command came from one of the sailors: "Wash!"

Shivering against the breeze, Aia scrubbed the blood and dirt off her skin. The cold water snapped her out of the haze—only then did she realize how caked in grime she'd become. How many warrior's blood had spilled onto her flesh? Another cold splash of water was poured over her head. Her breath hitched, a flicker of defiance sparking in her eyes. A cold wave washed over her, stiffening her limbs. She dropped the cloth onto the deck. The hot sun began to dry her skin. The sailor turned her around again to face the Carthaginian, who allowed a small smile to creep into his cold face.

He tilted his head, admiring her beauty. "Much better," he said. "Perhaps you should have sold me that sword when you had the chance."

Aia didn't give him the satisfaction of a response.

Baalhaan pointed to the opening in the deck and the sailors pushed her towards it. She climbed down into a long hallway filled with lines of warriors sitting on benches, rowing the ship. The guards propelled her through a second opening that led to another lower deck. A row of cages filled with men and women lined the long hallway. After cutting her bonds, she was thrust into the largest cage at the end of the passage. A single captive was in the cell, silent. As the iron-barred door slammed shut behind her, she turned to look at her captors as they walked away. She clasped the cold iron bars, and listened to the steady thrust of oars as they passed through the water, accompanied by a drum beat which marked the beginning of her enslavement.

A familiar voice came from the other prisoner in the cell. "Princess Aia!"

When she turned around, she saw General Hilerno, beaten and bloody, standing in the cell. Worry showed in the lines of a face that had always been filled with arrogance. Though she submitted to his embrace, she did not return it. Hilerno took a step back, dropped his arms and glowered at her. "I do not understand you."

Aia turned away from him and lay hold of the iron bars again. "When I fight I forget," she said. "But then I come to myself and what I've done terrifies me."

"What are you talking about?"

"My skill as a warrior has only brought grief," she said. "I have become a barbarian."

"You're the same as you ever were," he said. "A deceiver with enticing words and a thief's manner. A cold manipulator without honor."

Aia didn't respond, feeling the fire of anger rise in her heart.

"Oh, I don't mean to criticize you, princess. I admire your desire to win at any price."

A wish to slip into the shadows grew inside Aia's heart. To disappear entirely, to go away into the night. She gripped the iron bars tightly, wishing she could break them.

"So you only have eyes for good men," he taunted. "What happened to your good man, princess?"

"Stop it, Hilerno."

"Your good man refused to go to war," said Hilerno, "so you flirted with me to make him jealous. You pushed him into trying to become a great man. What did he do?"

"Shut up."

"Karbelos chose to fight, didn't he?"

This time, she shouted, "Shut up!"

"Where is he now?"

Aia closed her eyes, clutching cold iron, not wanting to remember.

Hilerno came up behind Aia and turned her around gently. His words were a whisper out of a nightmare. "Where is your prince?"

Aia shoved him back. "He's dead!"

"Dead with honor and glory," whispered Hilerno, "and still you reject me."

Leaning against the iron bars, Aia slipped down to the floor as a flood of tears poured from her eyes. She had destroyed a truly good man. The man she had fallen in love with. Her heart was beating wildly, but after a time, it settled down to match the cold drumbeats that came from their captors. A cold rhythm that led only into darkness.

* * *

The warship sailed downriver to Celsa, a Sedetani fortress built on the terraces that overlooked the waterway. The Iber river had become a valuable trade route which connected Iberia to the rest of the world. Merchant ships were loaded with wine to send downriver while foreign luxuries arrived on Carthaginian ships from across the sea. The Melqart remained docked at Celsa for a day and then got underway again, heading into a series of lakes which connected the upper and lower Iber rivers.

One day, Aia sat in the cell listening to the rowers move in time with the steady drumbeats while trying to ignore Hilerno, who had grown silent. She had not cooperated with her captors and they had placed an iron ring around her neck that was attached to the wall with a chain. They had also bound her wrists with iron shackles. Hilerno was not bound at all.

"You shouldn't fight them," he said.

"I will always fight them," said Aia.

The clinking sounds of a key chain made her look. A pair of guards opened the cell door. Tyresius stepped into the cell. Aia noticed Lilura standing in the hallway with a sullen look on her face. Tyresius made a motion to one of the guards. "Release her."

Aia raised her eyebrows and held her hands aloft for the guard to open the shackles that bound her hands together. After she was free, she stood up and threw her arms round Tyresius. Aia whispered in his ear, "I'm so glad to see you, master."

Tyresius smiled. "So, you have accepted me."

She lied. "Yes, master." Aia dropped her eyes down to the wood deck. "I am your gift. I am yours and you are mine."

Tyresius seemed satisfied. He motioned towards the cell door. "Come."

Aia tilted her head slightly and brushed a strand of blonde hair out of her eyes. "Tell me, what would have happened if I had opened the Magic Jar?"

"All of the god's blessings and curses for humanity would escape," he said. "All that would remain would be man's free choice. This would control his fate." Tyresius gave her a stern look. "In any case, the magic seal cannot be broken while I am alive."

"Oh," she said. "That is good."

Aia nodded and went out of the cell. Lilura glared at her with unconcealed hatred. Ignoring the Seer, Aia walked past, followed by Tyresius. As soon as he had turned his back to Lilura, the woman screamed. Aia turned around and saw Tyresius slumping to the floor with a knife in his back. Lilura grabbed a spear out of the hands of one of the surprised warriors. Lilura threw it at Aia, who was still too shocked to get out of the way.

Hilerno leaped in front of Aia, taking the spear full in the chest. With a groan he fell to the ground. One of the warriors grabbed Lilura, who screamed. Aia stared at the enraged woman until she had quieted down. "How could you do that? How could you betray someone you love?"

Lilura didn't answer. The fire in her eyes made Aia want to turn away. Lilura dropped her gaze down to Tyresius, who lay on the deck while a pool of blood formed around him. Lilura began to cry. Her sobs turned to agony. Aia felt a pang of guilt, knowing that her deception had caused this.

The second warrior pointed a spear at Aia and she went back into the cell. The door clanged shut and she knelt onto the deck, clutching the iron bars. Hilerno gave her a final glance and smiled.

Aia looked into his eyes. "Why?"

"You are my queen," he said. "I am sorry that you lost the man you loved, princess."

Aia bit her lip, unable to say anything.

A moment later, the light in his eyes went out.

* * *

Night had come with the cold. Aia sat in her cell, shivering. No shackles bound her hands together. She had simply been forgotten—no more than a valuable piece of cargo to sell at the next port. Down the hallway, a light appeared, accompanied by the sounds of two men talking in a foreign tongue. It was not Punic, the language of the Carthaginians, but something else. Aia had heard it before. As the two men approached, she remembered similar words spoken by her father's adviser. It was the Attic-Ionic language of the Hellenes, which she understood.

Aia's heart was filled with relief at the sight of Aristæus, who walked next to Baalhaan. She smiled at him. "Aristæus—you have come to ransom me."

Aristæus did not reply. He did not even acknowledge her presence.

Baalhaan spoke in a bored tone. "I am in a dreadful mood. Why have you brought me down here, Aristæus?"

"To show you," he said, "that beauty is the great seducer of men."

"I really don't know what you're talking about," said Baalhaan.

Aristæus smiled at his adversary, Baalhaan. "Culchas would have killed this girl if he had not been entranced by her beauty."

"So?"

"So, I beat you," said Aristæus, "when she destroyed the Sedetani army."

"Yes, yes, very well," grumbled Baalhaan. He withdrew a single silver coin and handed it to Aristæus. The image on the coin was that of an owl. "Our wager is over. Your barbarians were stronger than mine this time."

Aristæus had a look of triumph on his face. Aia had never seen him smile like that. It was like the first light of summer on a spring morning, after the winter snows had melted. "Where is the rest?"

Baalhaan looked thoroughly demoralized. "Fine." He withdrew the black stone which Aia had seen in his hand and he gave it to Aristæus, who pressed it against the white stone in his hand.

Aia let out a hiss. "This was only a game to you?"

The two glanced at her, but only momentarily.

Aia spoke up again to draw their attention. "Our two peoples have fought and bled and died," she said, "and you were the ones that instigated this war, as a simple amusement?"

Aristæus had a look of irritation on his face. "You're a barbarian," he said. "You're too primitive to understand the way we think."

"My father was wrong about you, Aristæus."

Aristæus turned away to leave.

Aia's words were soft but they brought him to a stop. "Before you came to civilize us, we had no prisons with iron bars like these. No criminals lived among us, only those without honor. We did not mint coins and had no money, so a person's worth could not be determined by it. If someone needed help, we gave them what they needed."

Aristæus scoffed at her words. "Charity is no substitute for progress."

Aia shrugged. "We valued the exchange of love. The only thing which is great in this world is kindness."

Aristæus grumbled, "The fate of inferior barbarians is unimportant."

"Oh yes, your people are truly civilized." taunted Aia, "but my people will no longer bleed for your entertainment."

"Where has your love brought you?" asked Aristæus. Amusement grew into a smile and he turned to Baalhaan. "I swear by all the gods of Olympus, love shall kill us all one day."

Turning away from them both, Aristæus walked away, laughing to himself. Baalhaan threw an irritated, defeated look at Aia and followed his rival out while she lingered by the gateway that led to her own darkened soul.

* * *

A hot day warmed the wood decks of the Melqart. Aia emerged from the hatch that led from the lower decks into a bright sunny day. She raised chained hands up to shield her eyes from the sunlight and cast a gaze all around the warship in wonder. Nothing but water stretched out in every direction. A slight breeze blew her hair into her face. A large island in the distance was shrouded by clouds that rested upon a mountain. One of her captors yanked her chains. Aia was brought to the open tent at the aft of the ship. Though the Magic Jar was nowhere to be seen, she could see Baalhaan reclining on a couch next to a table laden with food. An imperious attitude, passive and at the same time, superior, dictated all of his actions. He motioned to the tall Carthaginian guard. "Release her."

"Pardon, my lord?"

"Let her go. Remove those chains."

To her surprise, the warrior unlocked her shackles.

Baalhaan watched her closely as her restraints were removed. He glanced at the soldier and waved a hand. "Now, go away."

Aia watched the man retreat ten paces out into the sunshine. With a bow, he returned below the main deck.

Baalhaan gestured towards a cushioned seat. "You may sit."

The heavy weight of shackles gone, Aia rubbed the pain away from her wrists and sat down opposite Baalhaan. The sun was going down.

"Eat."

Aia didn't wait for another invitation. She tore a leg off a roasted chicken and began to devour it. With her other hand, she picked up a handful of dates and looked at them curiously.

"Careful," he warned. "Dates are sweet on the outside but they have a hard pit."

Aia shrugged and began to eat them carefully.

"How many days has it been?" he asked.

Through a mouthful of food, she responded, "How many days since what?"

"Your enslavement."

"Oh," Aia put down the bare chicken bone and picked up a cup of wine, drinking deeply from it before giving an answer. "Ten days, I think."

"You're not curious to know where we're taking you?"

"I hadn't thought about it," she lied. In truth, she didn't really care what happened to her anymore, but she was always curious. The rowers had stopped several days ago and the ship bounced up and down but always moved forward, propelled by sails. She wondered if they were going to one of the Punic colonies along the coasts of

198

Iberia, or even headed to the shining city of Carthage itself.

Baalhaan pointed beyond the tent opening, towards the island. "That is the island of Atalayassa. On the other side of that mountain lies the city of Ebusos. That is where Culchas has gone."

Aia stopped eating.

"He has taken the Magic Jar to a hidden cave," said Baalhaan. "You will find the entrance to it along the coast there."

"Why tell me?"

Baalhaan's face remained impassive, but she could feel the his heart burning. Perhaps he wanted to get back at Aristæus. His next words surprised her. "You are free to go."

"What?"

"I am granting you freedom." Baalhaan pointed to a bundle next to the table, "You might want to take your sword with you."

Aia retrieved the sword of Auruningica, made sure it was secure and slung it over her back. "Why are you helping me?"

"Because it amuses me."

Aia got up and went out of the tent. With a run, she jumped off the deck of the ship and plunged down into the cold seawater. She swam on and on underwater and came up for air some distance away from the warship. She saw sailors along the deck raising the anchor and climbing up to the rigging to unfurl the sails. Turning away from the Bireme, she looked at the beach and began to swim towards it.

* * *

The warm embrace of the man she loved filled her with joy. She wanted to hold him, to keep on holding him forever. Karbelos let go and stepped back. His armor shone in the sunlight and he carried a steel helmet in one hand. The white feathered plume brushed his face. His smile was the last she would ever see.

"Don't go."

Karbelos smiled. "I have to, Aia. Like you said, I have to defend my people."

"I will join you," she said, "once the contingent of warriors from my father have arrived. Though I would rather fight at your side."

"Don't worry." Karbelos put his helmet on. "We shall quickly brush the Sedetani army aside and then we can be together, forever."

Karbelos waved goodbye and got onto his white horse. As he rode away towards his men, she finally let the tears come. She shook her head and wondered aloud, "What have I done?"

* * *

Night had come. The tide washing up onto the beach covered up Aia's footprints. Inhaling the salty air, Aia approached the cave entrance. When she drew near, she hid behind a large boulder and peered over it. Ten Sedetani warriors stood guard. She sat down with her back to the rock, wondering if she could beat them all. Closing her eyes, she whispered a prayer to the The Supreme Mothers and then spoke aloud, "To victory."

Drawing her sword, Aia stepped out from behind the rock.

She cut three of them down before they could react. Recovering from his surprise, a tall soldier came on, sword in hand. She thrust her sword. He tried to parry it but she was too fast and impaled him. She put her foot on his chest and pulled her sword out. Swift footsteps came towards her. Whirling around, Aia blocked a strike and slashed back, cutting the Sedetani's head off. A fierce sword strike was aimed at her head and she dodged out of the way. The man's sword struck the rock behind her. Aia looked into the faces of the remaining five soldiers. Two of them broke off and ran away down the beach.

Their leader glanced after them, furious. As he called out to his men, she struck him square in the chest. The man to his side aimed a mace at her head and she ducked under it. Aia kicked him in the chest and he fell back onto the sand. The final soldier hesitated. Gripping a short sword in his hand, he glanced at his dead companions. Anger spilled into his eyes as he slashed out several times. Aia retreated, while parrying all of his attacks. The second man got up and joined in the assault. Aia ran away, around a large rock. She stopped, turned around and waited. Aia cut them down one at a time as they ran after her.

Panting, Aia listened to the seabirds. Their cries were nearly drowned out by the waves crashing onto the beach. A smile slipped into her face. She had won. The cave entrance was a pool of shadows that lay before her. Aia went inside.

* * *

The walls had closed in around her. No light guided her progress, but there was only one way to go: Forward. A slight breeze whistled through the passage. A whisper came along with it, like a rider on a horse. The word was too faint to distinguish clearly. Aia had to crawl through the passage, which seemed to go on for ages. The sounds of the ocean waves had long ago faded away and the cave passage became silent, except for the occasional whisper on the breeze, which came on like a slow heartbeat. It turned out to be a single word, still too quiet to recognize. Aia wondered if it came from the spirit inside the mountain. As she moved on the call came again, louder this time. Now the word was clear, "Freedom!"

The sound of dripping water grew louder and all at once, the small passage opened up onto a grotto. Bright moonlight fell down from an opening high up in the roof of the cave. Aia stood upright, stretched and cast her gaze around the wide chamber. A cold blast of air blew down from the wide opening in the roof and with it, the whisper. "Freedom!"

The opening in the roof was quite large. Sunlight fell down onto a dark oak tree growing in the center of the cave. No bird nested there among its dark branches. Green leaves constantly shivered, though there was no breeze at all inside the massive chamber. A stone altar stood at the base of the tree, which wrapped a large root around it, as if it was cradling the stone. Every limb of the tree was stained with blood. To the side of the chamber a pit filled with bodies brought forth a terrible stench. Serpents twined round the limbs. Next to the altar rested the Magic Jar. Culchas stood there, bare chested, with a bloody knife in one hand. The corpse of a young boy was upon the stone, having just given up his life. The single cry from a sacred bird came down from the higher branches of the tree, ready to take the child's spirit up into the sky.

Aia wrinkled her nose at the dark grotto and drew her sword, still blood-stained from the fight at the cave mouth. The fallen god called out to her from inside his prison, "Freedom!"

Culchas put the knife down and picked up a steel sword, no doubt pillaged from the battle with her people. "So, you have come."

"Yes," she glanced at the Magic Jar. "The fallen god calls to me."

"You and I are alike," he said. "You seek vengeance, just as I have done."

"Come on," she taunted. "Play with me."

Culchas stepped out onto the floor of the cave. Aia jumped forward and delivered a downward blow. He blocked it and swung at her chest. Aia blocked it, but the force of his blow knocked her back and she fell down.

Culchas grinned. "The fallen god has given me great strength. You cannot defeat me."

"There is more to a fight than strength." Aia jumped to her feet. She nodded to the bodies of the sacrificial victims. "Why did you kill them?"

The Carthaginians taught me to do this," he said. "They make sacrifices to their god Baal and they are granted great powers."

"What of Neito, your war god?"

"Neito has failed me, as did my high priest, Orisos, when you killed him." Culchas swung his sword and a flame came out of the blade, casting firelight into the walls of the cave.

Aia jumped out of the way and faced him again, only to dodge another attack, accompanied by a jet of fire. She retreated a few paces. The fires had startled her. "Why have you come here?"

Culchas raised his sword, which was covered in flames. Fire danced over moonlight. "I will imprison the fallen god here, away from everyone. I have enough strength already to build an empire. "No longer will I tolerate interference."

She glanced at the Magic Jar. "Why not open it?"

"I'm not so curious." He aimed a series of attacks at her and Aia had to dodge them all, rolling out of the way. Culchas ran forward and grabbed her by the throat. He threw her like a rag doll cast aside by an angry child. When Aia slammed against the cave wall it knocked the wind out of her. Culchas aimed a fiery strike at her heart.

Aia parried the blow and moved away from the wall. She tried striking him with a series of attacks, but he blocked them all easily, laughing.

Aia retreated but he did not follow. Culchas had a triumphant look on his face. She took up a fighting stance and held her sword out in front.

Culchas laughed again.

Aia looked at the Magic Jar. "Apollyon, how would you like to be free?"

Culchas's laughter died away and he looked at her in surprise. Aia called out to the fallen god, "Burn him."

All at once Culchas was engulfed in a pillar of flames. His death throes filled the cavern with cries of defiance. Spite turned to agony. Aia stood there and watched him burn until the light became too bright. After he was gone, she whispered, "I'm not at all like you."

Closing her eyes, Aia remembered Karbelos, smiling at her as he rode away into battle. "A good person must be ruthless in the defense of those they love. With your passing, the old fires of hate shall fade away from this world."

* * *

Morning sunshine touched her face as she emerged from the mouth of the cave, carrying the Magic Jar. A salty breeze greeted Aia as she knelt down on the beach, placing the fallen god there under the warm light. Over the rolling sounds of the tide washing in, she could hear a single albatross call out a lonely cry. She glared at the Magic Jar. "You are just like the Hellenes and the Carthaginians. You have used the tyranny of kindness, the granting of wishes, in order to manipulate people into acts of barbarity and cruelty."

In answer, a whisper returned from the Magic Jar and mingled with the sounds of the tides washing in. It was only a single word: "Freedom!"

Aia sat down onto her heels and wondered aloud, "Perhaps we should all be content with what the gods give us, whether it is good fortune or grievous fates."

The wax seal around the rim of the lid was cracked and worn. She ran her hands down the sides of the amphora jar, wondering at the cruelty of mankind, but there was great kindness there, too.

204

She looked at the artwork along the sides. It reminded her of the night she had seen the god as he fell out of heaven, to light up the skies brighter than the sun.

A passing cloud cast its shadow over the beach, engulfing her in darkness. With one hand, Aia lifted the lid of the amphora jar. The ground shook. A thunderclap came from the heavens, and a single bolt of lightning came down. Aia was knocked onto her back, even as a great whooshing sound swirled around her like a stormy gale. Rising to look, she could see thousands of brightly colored butterflies emerging from the amphora jar. As they flew into the heavens, some of them turned to gold, while others had black wings decorated with beautiful colors. Aia crawled towards the amphora jar. The rising crescendo of light and dark thinned out until only a single golden butterfly remained. Picking up the lid, Aia placed it back on top, to seal in a final blessing. To her amazement, she saw that the wax seal reformed around the lid.

The cloud drifted away and sunlight shone down onto the beach once again. Aia brushed a strand of hair out of her face. "Our destinies will come from the free choices that we make, not from the gods."

Aia sat down on the beach and looked at the rising sun. She let her eyes drift into the sea. "This is going to change everything."

THE END

MARK O'BANNON
Biography

Mark O'Bannon is an American novelist, screenwriter, and game designer best known as the author of the science fiction series *Imperium* and for three fantasy series: *Whiskers, Aia the Barbarian,* and *Shadows and Dreams.*

O'Bannon is the CEO of Shadowstar Games, which publishes the Interactive Storytelling Game (a Pen & Paper Role Playing Game), "Fantasy Imperium."

O'Bannon is an advocate of Self-Publishing and teaches workshops to aspiring authors on how to publish, market and promote their work.

Born in San Diego, California, O'Bannon is the grandson of the famous aviation pioneer, Reuben H. Fleet (who acquired the Wright Brother's airplane company Dayton-Wright along with Gallaudet Aircraft and formed Consolidated Aircraft, the makers of the famous B-24 Liberator bombers and the PB-Y Catalina flying boats from WWII).

O'Bannon is a registered Libertarian and runs a non-profit, Mapping Freedom, which teaches Free World Theory (FWT), an exploration of the freedoms protected by the U.S. Constitution, and new scientific discoveries of freedom, coercion, property, slavery and intellectual property.

www.ingramcontent.com/pod-product-compliance
Lightning Source LLC
Chambersburg PA
CBHW050526260626
47157CB00004B/1485